Anne Keens

Molly Munday's Cupcakes

First published in Great Britain in 2024

Typesetting and publishing by UK Book Publishing.

www.ukbookpublishing.com

ISBN: 978-1-917329-37-8

I would like to dedicate my novel to a beloved sister
Carol Jean

My heart felt thanks firstly to the very talented Melissa Esme for her beautiful illustrations and front cover design. I am overwhelmed by her generosity of this gift. (melissaesme.co.uk)

Secondly a thank you to my family for their help and guidance due to my very basic IT skills and especially to Keith for his proof reading.

Lastly a thank you to Richard for his encouragement and tolerance over the many hours I have spent working on this novel.

A Fresh Start

Chapter 1

S leep deprivation was not an uncommon occurrence for Molly at this time in her life.

The number representing her age in years was going to reach the half century at her next birthday. This thought was never far from her mind. The previous decade had simply flown by. Molly's busy lifestyle, a combination of work and leisure time with far more emphasis on her leisure time had meant she had persistently overindulged in everything deemed to be (bad for your health) and she had never given a toss.

Molly passionately believed that the excessive amount of money that her husband had often accused her of spending on expensive beauty products and treatments had been worthwhile and had prevented signs of aging on the outside.

It was however on the inside of her body that things were beginning to feel noticeably different, and she knew it had been only a matter of time when she like most women of her age would join the dreaded menopausal club.

It had been just three years ago when Molly became aware of the subtle changes within her body. It had started with the sporadic stop-start bleeding happening in her monthly periods. At first, she thought to herself if this was all that was going to happen then so be it "I can cope easily, Bring it on!" But now things were hotting up! Literally. Molly knew it was time for major lifestyle changes.

There had been an increasing number of wakeful interludes on this and preceding nights where she found herself entangled in the damp bed sheets. Molly's sexy silky night garments had long been cast aside in exchange for the more modest cotton ones that she now chose to wear. Just occasionally Molly would revert to a more glamorous attire when she was feeling amorous and wanted to please or tease her husband. But this, she was aware, was also becoming less frequent.

The polka dot patterned cotton fabric nightshirt she was wearing had multiple creases due to her restlessness where she had continuously tossed and turned throughout the night. The garment was now sticking to her hot and sweaty body. It had become tangled and had risen above her waist where it had caused a tightness which had led to soreness under her small but what her husband had often referred to as her perfect breasts.

Throwing the duvet off to let out the heat had momentarily helped. Molly pulled at her nightshirt, straightening it out before retrieving the duvet quickly as her body rapidly cooled just as a blast of air blew in through the open window. Molly shivered, pulling once again at her nightdress, so the length hugged at her knees. She moved her body to a curled foetal position and desperately tried but as usual failed to get back to any resemblance of sleep.

Molly wondered if other people could vividly recall their dreams like she could.

"Perhaps one day when I have nothing better to do in my spare time, I will write a book" she thought.

Then again, she wondered, whether her readers would believe her? Especially the bizarre dream of this past night when she had found herself standing almost naked on a stage wearing only a throng of small black feathers and a headdress of larger purple ones which she had attached to her long blond curly wig. The auditorium she was standing in had been crowded with people, shouting, and cheering her on as she completed her song and dance routine whilst doing a striptease.

Molly recognised faces in the audience. Friends and acquaintances from the present and some that had crept in from her past which she now thought most bizarre. Molly recalled faces of local people from the village as well as customers. The friends from her past were ones she no longer stayed connected with save the odd ones she had sent annual Christmas cards to, having received one from them and which made her feel duty bound to send one back to.

In front of this full house, she had been singing a medley of catchy chorus songs. Now, Molly was not known to have the kind of singing voice that she could boast about, but she could sing in tune, and when encouraged to, after having drunk more than two large glasses of wine, she was known to take to the floor and sing along to the odd karaoke. But this had been her limit to pertaining any thoughts of ever being considered as (one who had talent that was worth pursuing)

Suddenly the audience one by one began rising to their feet shouting for an encore as she took her final bow stark naked. The lyrics of the final song would stay with Molly for the remainder of that day.

"Those were the days my friend, we thought they'd never end, we'd sing and dance forever and a day ….

Humming the tune and stretching her limbs having given up on any chance of ever getting back to sleep, Molly allowed herself a little chuckle as she recalled the red-faced Gary Thompson, son, and trainee of the village butcher renowned for his superb muscular body. From being a skinny teenager, he had often been the subject of teasing so had taken up body building. Gary now spent much of his leisure time in the gym. Supervising others as well as working out himself.

Gary had removed his bloodstained, blue-striped butcher's apron. With his shirt too tight for his six-pack torso and bulging biceps he was pushing forward through the crowd and like a true knight was trying to save?? Molly's dignity.

"Not sure I will be able to look the friendly butcher in the face anytime soon" Molly thought, smiling to herself.

Chapter 2

"Mol, are you awake yet love?" calls a familiar voice shouting from the bottom of the stairs.

"How could I be anything else" she thought to herself, startled by a loud crashing sound that came from somewhere below stairs causing her to finally wake to a fuller state of comprehension.

"Yes, dear, I'm awake" she responds with a sigh.

The aroma of freshly made coffee wafted up the stairs and filled her nostrils. She smiled to herself as she stretched her limbs and brought her body to a sitting position and then waited with eager anticipation. Molly loved her coffee especially the first cup of the day.

The sound of footsteps on the stairs and the clinking of mugs upon a tray was getting closer to her. Molly turned her body to pull and rearrange the pillows behind her back for support, such was her eagerness to be ready.

Dr Foster had suggested that she should consider reducing her intake of caffeine as she had confessed to him at her last appointment that her menopausal symptoms were becoming less tolerable but this advice she could not and would not consider.

Her husband Simon, on reaching the opened door, was already apologising for breaking one of the four china mugs that Iris had bought Molly for Christmas. The mugs beautifully decorated with colourful hens of various breeds including one of a Rhode Island hen and had been the breed that Simon and Molly had kept in their garden. The free-range eggs were invaluable for making the cake mix for the now growing ever more popular cupcakes.

Simon sat on the side of their bed and handed Molly a steaming mug of coffee. Placing the tray on the bedside table he sat on the edge of the bed swinging his legs on to the bed so he too could enjoy his beverage with his wife.

"I will get you a replacement, I know where Iris bought them from as I remember seeing them in Goddards window display before Christmas. May even be in the sale now so might be worth getting a couple more, just in case" he adds with a cheeky grin. Molly felt cross but held her tongue not wanting to start her day with a quarrel.

Molly sipped the hot liquid from one of her new mugs and soon began to feel more like herself and almost ready to face the day ahead.

"Sorry Si about last night" Molly says caressing Simon's hand.

"It's all right my love, I know you must have been tired after the party. I shouldn't have even suggested it" says Simon lifting Molly's hand to kiss it.

It was not that she had felt particularly tired, it was just that she had not wanted to have sex. Molly was happy on this occasion to let him believe this time that she had been too tired.

"Anyway, I'm off now, unless there is anything else you need me to do" he said tantalisingly, insinuating that she might like to consider having sex now.

"No that's ok" Molly replies hastily. "Best I get up as lots to do today."

Simon smiled as he bent to plant a kiss on her forehead before rising to leave.

"I've done the chickens, no eggs though" Simon continues and then bent over to plant another quick kiss, this time on her lips. "Love you lots Mol."

Molly had forgotten momentarily the reason he had got up so early that morning.

"Enjoy your golf love, say hello to Rob for me" and with that he was gone.

No longer savouring her coffee, Molly gulped down the remaining cooling liquid, knowing full well that there would be more in the kitchen downstairs. She had however also momentarily forgotten what else was waiting for her attention below stairs.

Molly shivered as she got out of bed. Her feet felt cold. Hurriedly she went into the bathroom. The warm heated floor was a luxury that she enjoyed. Stripping off her nightdress to place it in the washing basket she caught sight of her naked body in the mirror. "Not bad for a woman of my age" she remarks to herself, pulling in her tummy muscles and stretching her body to a less slouching posture.

She stepped into the hot power shower and let the water flow over her body before washing herself with her favourite perfumed gel. An expensive luxury and one that Simon had put in her Christmas stocking. Turning off the water she stepped out and quickly wrapped herself in a warm towel.

She turned to open the bathroom cupboard which displayed a concoction of natural herbal remedies. Fingering through the bottles and boxes she read aloud their contents before deciding which one she thought she might like to try this day.

"Now let me see, Black cohosh a member of the buttercup family" she read aloud. "I think I will give this one a go. How lucky I am to have so many thoughtful friends" she said smiling to herself.

At least half a dozen boxes and bottles filling her cabinet, she had bought on recommendation of friends, and she had bought these just to please them. Four bottles she observed, had been gifts given to her as alternatives to try.

The ones in the front she had bought herself from the health food shop after sharing her distressing symptoms with Tracey the shop assistant who she thought could not have been more than thirty years old herself. Unless of course she was one of those lucky ones who looked younger than she really was. Molly could never bring herself to enquire. Not that she did not want to know. Molly had occasionally tried to drop hints by complimenting her.

"What lovely skin you have Tracey" Molly had said to her on one occasion and on another visit to the shop "I love your new hair colour Tracey. It really suits you."

"Thank you, Molly. So, kind of you to say" she would respond before going into a selling mode by advising Molly on a particular brand or other that she believed was the best or latest on the market and that she should try.

Tracey accepted all the compliments but never in all the time Molly knew her had she ever divulged her age.

Molly believed that no one could know what it was like to live with the menopause unless they themselves were going through it or had come out the other side.

So it was that Molly thought Tracey's bathroom cupboard would contain sanitary pads and tampons just like hers used to. And a couple of boxes of painkillers for good measure as well.

Molly was not sure yet which of the two female curses would turn out to be the worst to put up with, monthly periods or the menopause. Or indeed which one was the most expensive to live with.

Chapter 3

It had been a family tradition to take down the tree on the 6th of January ending the Christmas festivities, however friends from the night before who had attended the impromptu twelfth night party had insisted that they would do this before they left. There had been no point in trying to convince their guests who had all had far too much to drink that this was not necessary. They had been insistent. They had been adamant it was going to be their way of saying thanks for a lovely evening.

As she entered the lounge Molly's demeanour changed from one of positive thoughts for the day to one of despair. The room was a mess, and the odour of last night's curry lingered more than a little. The Christmas tree was lying on the floor sparse of baubles and its needles which she could see strewn across the room. Partially eaten plates of food had remained left on the table. Glasses containing dregs and party decorations were everywhere she looked. In one corner of the room Molly spied the angel tree topper which had up until now sat proudly on top of the Christmas tree. It was sitting on one of the armchairs propped up by a cushion. In between its straddled legs was an empty whisky bottle. The golden sparkle halo had slipped from its wobbly head and had slid down the side of its face. The angel looked drunk.

Molly, treading carefully through the mess, headed towards the kitchen and the first aid box.

She took out a packet of paracetamol tablets and swallowed two down with a large glass of orange juice taken from the refrigerator. Turning towards the coffee percolator she saw there was sufficient coffee ready. She poured a mug full, downing the not so hot beverage before pouring a second one to empty the container of a not so fresh coffee. Molly became high on caffeine and was as ready as she could be under the circumstances for the task of clearing up the mess.

Molly had no one to blame but herself.

"Of course, I can manage" she insisted when Simon had offered to forfeit his round of golf to stay at home to help her with the clean-up following the aftermath of the merrymaking that they and their friends had enjoyed.

But that was last night when they had both retired to bed feeling merry and intoxicated, after they had both consumed several glasses of wine as well as a concoction of other alcoholic drinks over the course of the evening.

Once she got herself moving, it did not take Molly long however to get the house straight. She worked methodically and fast. The tree needles she knew would be more difficult to deal with having been trodden deep into the carpet pile by those guests that had been dancing. She realised the smell of beer and stale food would linger too, for the remainder of that day and no doubt the next.

"Time to put the percolator back on before I tackle the kitchen" she thought to herself, excited about the prospect of a well-earned fresh cup, or more likely two cups of coffee.

On the kitchen sideboard were three boxes of chocolates. The unopened lids displayed colourful, enticing pictures of their contents. Molly's guests had left a scattering of sweet wrappers strewn across her kitchen table and the kitchen floor.

Nobody could love chocolate more than Molly did. This was her third favourite consumable delight after coffee and red wine. All of which, her doctor had advised, she should try to cut down her consumption of because of her menopausal symptoms.

Removing the lids Molly viewed the disappointingly few remaining chocolates at the bottom of all three boxes. Fingering the sweets, she was not at all surprised to see that they were all the same flavours. Each box contained two or three strawberry creams, a couple of orange creams a few pieces of vanilla fudge and to her surprise her favourite coffee delights. Obviously not everyone else's favourite, Molly thought, as there were more of those left. As it was no longer worth keeping the boxes for so few chocolates, she emptied the contents of each into a small bonbon dish and discarded the boxes into the recycle bin. Sitting at the kitchen table with her fresh mug of coffee Molly's fingers began to play with the dish containing its mouth-watering contents.

Not having had any breakfast she felt ready to eat something. Knowing only full well that a high fibre cereal or a banana would be more beneficial for her alcohol-abused body from the evening before she had an overwhelming desire to taste the chocolate. Having no will power she picked up the strawberry cream. She unwrapped the sweet and placed it into her mouth creating an unusual amount of natural saliva as her taste buds took over. The mastication began and the pleasurable feeling was satisfying. Having now eaten the first and then the second, she continued until she had greedily consumed the lot.

Molly had always considered herself lucky in the fact that she never seemed to put on any weight, no matter how many calories she consumed. She thought this was not just due to having a high metabolism but also because she was constantly on the go.

It had been just six days ago when in the company of friends, she and Simon had celebrated bringing in the New Year. Molly, like many of her friends when under the influence of too much alcohol and on an evening that held so much emotional as well as celebratory positive feelings, had made her new year resolution.

In a slurring and loud speech Molly made a proclamation stating that this new year she would try to live a healthier lifestyle reducing both sugar and fat in her diet and drinking less coffee and alcohol.

She was not the only one to do this as others in her group had followed suit with their own new year resolutions.

It was however Iris's speech that had caught everyone's attention when she vowed in a believable manner to stop fancying Tom Cutler. Everyone had just fell about laughing at this confession except that is Iris herself who started to cry.

"No one understands me!" she said, taking tissues from her sleeve to wipe away her tears and blow her nose.

Molly had tried to console her friend, thankful that the men including Iris's husband were at the bar and had not heard her. The following day at coffee break they both laughed as they recalled what Iris had confessed to.

"I really do not know what got into me. It must have been the booze talking. I hardly remember saying it." Embarrassed and red-faced, Iris was in denial as she chatted with her friend. "As if I could ever fancy anyone other than my Rob."

Feeling a little sick and more than just a little guilty Molly quickly disposed of the chocolate wrappers into the bin just as a loud knock at the back door, followed simultaneously by the entrance of her best friend and employee Iris.

"Morning Mol" an excitable chatty Iris greets her friend, "Just wondered if you wanted any help clearing up the mess? Great party as always, had a bit of a headache this morning though. Think I overdid the wine a bit. How are you feeling? Am I in time for coffee?"

"Thanks for the offer, Iris, but I am almost done! Pull up a chair, I was about to make a fresh pot, then we can have a natter." Molly answered whilst busying herself by filling the kettle and rinsing the coffee grains from the used mugs.

Molly and Iris had been friends for years and full working partners for just three months. Both had shared a common enjoyment and enthusiasm for baking.

Molly had been teaching part time at college until one day she had an idea to start a new business. She had loved teaching home economics, but baking was by far what she enjoyed the most.

Being the sole beneficiary of her late mother's will, she now had the funds to follow her passion in a new dynamic way. Although she had been heartbroken when her mum had passed away Molly knew that she would have approved of this new venture.

Simon had taken little convincing and was as excited as she was. It had been his idea to convert and enlarge the utility room into a separate domain for the sole purpose of producing the cupcakes. He purchased and hung a sign on the adjoining door from their kitchen naming the room (MOLLYS OFFICE).

It was during the alterations that Molly undertook an online course on an introduction to running a business. To start with she had no idea what was involved but was keen to learn and she studied hard. Lectures about sole trading, product liability and insurance, health and safety including food hygiene and first aid at work filled her head. With advice from the friendly bank manager, she learnt how to set up profit and loss accounts for HMRC.

Initially the cakes she baked were sold to the village cafés and bakery. Within three months and with extended advertising her client numbers had increased. Locally, customers began ordering for private parties and events. Never had she been so busy. It was time to consider employing someone to help in her new office and finding the right person was going to be easier than she had thought.

Iris had worked in the school catering business for over fifteen years. Although she enjoyed the work, it did not challenge her creative ability that she knew she had. When Molly offered Iris the chance to work for her, she did not have to give it a second thought. At last Iris would be able to use her talent in a way that she had always wanted to do. And so began the new working relationship. Molly would be responsible for the baking, maintaining the accounts as well as taking the orders. Iris would create the flavoured butter icing and sugar mouldings to decorate the cakes with. Within a fleeting time, MOLLY MUNDAY'S CUP CAKES became an established familiar name which extended throughout the village community and beyond.

Iris sipped her coffee admiring the new mug that she had bought as a set of four for her friend at Christmas.

"Lovely coffee, thanks" she remarks taking a sip from the mug and taking a seat at the table.

"I'm so glad we decided to take January off, aren't you?"

Although a satisfying taste Molly did feel ever so slightly guilty knowing she had drunk three cups that morning already.

"Oh yes definitely the best thing we could have done" she says.

"We had such a busy time leading up to Christmas it's good to take a break now and I have enjoyed myself this Christmas despite spending it on our own" she adds. "By the way Iris. Are you the one responsible for leaving my angel with a whisky bottle on her lap? Molly asks, smiling at her friend knowing full well it was.

Remembering the impish incident of last night, Iris chuckled and then burnt her lip as she was taking another sip of her hot drink.

"Oh! I forgot about that. I know I shouldn't tell tales, but it was really Si's fault, he put me up to it."

The friends giggled together as they often did as they deliberated over the successful party of the night before. Molly told Iris of the ludicrous dream that she had had, and this caused Iris to laugh more loudly.

"I'm glad I'm not the only one who has silly dreams and sometimes says ridiculous things" says Iris remembering what she had said on New Year's Eve.

"I know I can trust you Mol to say nothing so I will tell you about the dream I had the other night" says Iris giggling as she describes in detail the passionate session of love making with the vicar. "A bit like Lady Chatterley. Just it was a vicar instead of a gardener."

Odd, Molly thought to herself when they had both finished laughing, that Iris was owning up to dreaming about Tom for a second time. She wondered if indeed Iris did have feelings for the Reverend Thomas Cutler. She knew herself that he could be a bit flirtatious at times but dismissed this as a ludicrous thought.

"I won't be able to look at the vicar now without blushing and as for his wife, I dread to think what she would have made of it," says Iris.

Each knew that they could trust one another with anything that they discussed between them. Well almost anything.

They had spoken often on their experiences relating to the menopause. Quite often Iris would offer advice on natural remedies that she herself had taken. She was a firm believer in natural remedies for any ailment where Molly held different views on the subject, however she was always keen to try her friend's latest suggestion. "Anything," she would say if it worked and would give her some relief.

Conversation turned to their plans for the deep cleaning of the (office) and preparation for the year ahead. Orders were already coming in for the following month.

"Nearly forgot to tell you Mol" says Iris, "Rob thinks he may have found a suitable van for you. He will tell you more about it tonight."

"That is exciting news. I have been keeping my fingers crossed hoping for the right vehicle to come along. We really could do with our own transport now."

"Are you looking forward to going tonight" asks Iris getting up from the table. "What time shall we meet?"

Iris picks up both empty mugs and takes them across to the sink to wash up but not wanting Molly to know she has noticed the broken mug in the sink decided to leave them both on the side. She could hazard a guess that it was Si who had broken one of the new mugs as he could be a bit clumsy at times, and decided she would purchase another couple to replace them when she next goes shopping.

"Yes, I am really looking forward to it. Better get there early if we want to guarantee somewhere to sit. Shall we say seven thirty?" suggests Molly. "If for any reason Si is running late, I will give you a bell."

"Better wear something cool too, you know how hot it gets in the pub when the fire gets going" Iris teases whilst pretending to fan her face with her hand.

Chapter 4

It was twenty-five minutes past seven exactly when Molly and Simon entered the Old Harry's Arms. They quickly found a suitable table for four, not too close to the fire. They had been lucky as it was one of only two tables vacant at a comfortable distance from the already roaring log fire.

The eighteenth-century pub was once an old coaching inn. Originally it had a thatched roof. The thatch had since been replaced with tiles of the same period following a fire. Molly had been away at university at that time. Her mother had reported the incident to her and had sent her the local newspaper cuttings showing photos of the damage that had occurred. If it had not been for the quick response of the postal worker who had seen smoke coming from an upper floor window and called the fire brigade the damage might have been colossal. As it was, only one corner of the roof and one of the upper rooms were severely damage. Two of the other top floor rooms got away with smoke damage.

The pub which Molly had grown up with and had spent social time with friends in before she left the village had to close for more than a year for repairs. Molly returned home visiting her mother for the grand reopening and to meet the new owners.

The interior of Old Harrys Arms had retained all its rustic charm with low wood beams across the ceilings and an uneven flag stone floor. The bar furniture was made from a dark wood. The tables and chairs had a gothic appearance.

An assorted range of local photographs hung on the walls including one depicting the coaching inn and how it had looked before the fire. There was also a selection of photographs showing the before and after the fire incident. Next to these was a framed newspaper cutting with a photo of the local postal worker who had received special recognition for his quick response to the fire. He was receiving an award from the then proprietors.

Above the pictures were cluttered dusty rustic wooden shelves displaying various objects from past times. Molly and Iris had enjoyed trying to identify the more unusual pieces and trying to work out their uses, and if they did not have a clue one or the other would say:

"I expect Mum would have known what that had been used for" or "I think I remember seeing one of those when I was a child but to this day, I cannot remember what it had been used for."

They were both in agreement when they discussed the topic of cleaning of the implements.

"I don't know how the shelves stay up with all that clutter and look at all the cobwebs" Iris commented on one occasion to Molly.

"Yes, and how anyone could reach without a ladder is beyond me" she had replied.

Historical documents had shown that the one large room originally had been divided into three separate rooms, but now there were individual tabled areas with wood partitions and open upper frames. This allowed people to sit in small groups but at the same time gave the feeling of being in one room.

Old Harry's Arms was renowned for its excellent food. The current proprietors David and Sacha Armstrong had relocated from Yorkshire where they had been successfully managing public houses for a brewery. This pub however, they had bought freehold. The locals had welcomed the couple warmly into the village and looked on in anticipation as the renovation took place. What had once been a tired and shabby pub had become a popular place to gather and there were now times when booking a table for a meal became essential to avoid disappointment. The Armstrongs, keen to build up a good relationship with the village residents, had chosen to source ingredients from local businesses. They prided themselves on their culinary skills and produced a variety of delicious dishes. They were now not only running a successful and profitable business but supporting others in the village and this ensured their popularity.

This night however, there was no choice of food. Everyone would be offered a free meaty faggot shaped into a burger served in a bread roll as part of the traditional faggot burning charity evening. Molly had been prepared for this and both she and Simon had eaten the reheated leftover curry from the previous evening before coming out.

Simon went to the bar placing an order for two glasses of dry cider and two large glasses of red wine. He was greeted warmly by David who with his wife Sacha had been guests at their party the evening before.

"Thanks for last night, we really enjoyed ourselves."

From further down the bar, Sacha who was busy serving a growing number of customers caught Simon's eye. She smiled and winked at him.

"My Sacha had a few too many, had a bit of a sore head this morning" David added "but wouldn't admit to it."

"Same goes for Mol but she'd never admit to it either" replied Simon as he took out his wallet to pay for the drinks.

"These are on us; I think you deserve them for the mess I remember we left behind."

"Cheers David, we are pleased everyone had a wonderful time. I'm afraid I left Mol to clear up the mess and played golf with Rob."

The two friends exchanged a few more niceties before Simon moved away from the bar to allow another customer standing behind him to be served.

Scanning around the room it was obvious that the place was going to be packed this evening. As ever, he thought to himself, the tradition of faggot burning on the twelfth night had become more popular and more people were now attending from neighbouring villages.

It was several minutes before Simon returned to their table. He kept having to stop to chat when people recognised him. Molly was watching him and was waiting eagerly for her glass of wine. It was too noisy for her to hear the exchange of conversation which by Si's face had obviously included good humorous banter.

Ahead of him Simon could see that Iris and Rob had arrived and had taken their seats at the table. He could hear the laughter as he approached.

Rob stood up and helped himself from the tray of drinks thanking Simon as he did so.

"Don't thank me mate, David bought these" he says taking his seat next to Molly and explaining as he did so that the drinks had been on the house as a thanks for their party the night before.

Molly took a large gulp from her glass. She felt she had waited long enough. The smooth red wine slid warmly down her throat. Molly smiled contentedly.

"Cheers everyone" she says before taking a second gulp. Mmm… This wine tastes delicious. Not our usual one I don't think" she says to Iris who agrees.

"David opened a new bottle. He said he thought you would like it" says Simon.

Molly looked towards the bar and caught David's eye. Smiling she raised her glass and mouthed the word cheers. David smiling back mouthed the words "You're welcome."

The four friends were enjoying another fun evening together and were looking forward to the merriment to begin.

The custom of the burning of the ashen faggot had been reintroduced to the pub by David and Sacha. They had wanted to celebrate the lost or forgotten traditions that had once been popular in the rural areas of the west country. Their research had discovered that the origins were not well understood but believed by some historians to have been of a pagan nature.

George Brown, who owned and managed his farm on the outskirts of the village, had been extremely willing to allow one of his farmhands to put together the long length of the ashen faggot. He said it would be a good idea for (young Jack) as George had called his son for him to learn about the local tradition. Jack would however be handsomely paid for the work by the proprietors.

Having gathered the sticks, Jack worked the long bundle entwining them together before bounding it. Tying strips of willow and hazel as markers along the length of the completed faggot. Sprigs of holly were then attached at each marker. Jack had become exceptionally accomplished in his methods, producing a very pleasing result.

At eight o'clock Jack entered the bar to raucous cheers along with the banging of hands-on tables. The noise was deafening.

"Gangway" Jack shouts as he ceremoniously leads the way through the length of the room. His friends Stuart and Al were helping to carry the enormous faggot to where the fire was glowing red and orange with healthy flames. Jack placed the presenting part of the faggot carefully into the fire under the watchful eyes of his helpers. The remainder resting along the length of the floor. The fire crackled and spat out sparks of hot embers into the air and smoke bellowed up the chimney before settling into a more gentle and slower burning.

Jenny the bartender watched on checking that all was in order. Molly saw her whisper something in Jack's ear. Whatever she had said had made Jack blush. He responded by whispering something in Jenny's ear. This time it was Jenny's turn for her cheeks to turn pink and she started to giggle.

"If I didn't know any better, I would think there was something going on with that pair" Molly says to Iris "Look at them!

"I agree. Not noticed before but they do seem a bit more friendly towards each other."

Jenny had become more than just an employee when she came to work for her landlord. What started as a trial for Jenny when she initially started work with the Armstrongs had very quickly become a permanent job. She was now a valued employee and a resident member of the staff. She had progressed from those first few weeks of her new job when her tasks had been to help in the kitchen and perform house cleaning duties. These days however, Jenny would often be behind the bar serving customers and everyone loved her. Jenny was a friendly individual. She was full of confidence with no airs or graces. She spoke with an exaggerated local west country accent which tourists particularly enjoyed and she had a way of making everyone feel important. Best of all she was a colourful and flamboyant person and fun to be around.

On this night once again, Jenny was acting as a judge to the proceedings. With her oversized wristwatch and carrying a clip board and pen she was ready to function as timekeeper. She stood ready and watching as the burning commenced.

Jack along with his mates Al, one of the village's fire fighters, and his partner Stuart functioned as the fire monitors. They would ensure everyone's safety by keeping people at a safe distance. But it was Jack, who was proud of his work, whose job it was to push the bundle further into the fire as it burnt away.

All bets were made and the customary donations to the chosen charity of the occasion were collected in. This year the monies collected were to be shared between the local hospice and the new family centre that was due to open within the next couple of months. The winners would be those who had predicted the closest time nearest to each burnt section of the bundle. Their prizes of tiny amounts of money also taken from the overall betting cash.

The music was in full swing. Oli and his son Andy had once again been invited as paid musicians to entertain for the event. The duet played instruments and sang a repertoire of catchy songs with choruses that everyone if they felt inclined could join in with. Oli had been an amateur musician for years and had played in a local folk band but was now retired. His son Andy was a student and studied music. Simon knew both well and had taught Andy at college.

Molly was now sipping on her second glass of wine.

"Phew! Is it me or is it hotter than usual?" she asks as she picks up a beer mat and wafts it like a fan. Molly undid the two top buttons of her blouse.

"I'm getting a bit hot too, it's all right for men. They don't know what it's like" replies Iris having to raise her voice above the increasing pub din causing heads to turn in response.

With that Rob stood up and leaning over Iris opens the small window above them, while at the same time defending both his and Simon's understanding of the women's problems.

"Thanks Rob, I'm melting" then to Iris she says, "I think I'll come back as a man next time."

"Me too" said Iris catching Rob's eye.

"I do try to understand how you feel don't I love?" he says to Iris affectionately putting an arm around her shoulders.

"Same goes for me" says Simon, not wanting to sound any less caring of the women's problems.

"We are lucky to have the both of you. Aren't we Iris? says Molly trying to lighten the conversation and not sound too sarcastic.

Conversation switched to the subject of the vehicle that Rob had managed to find, and thought would be suitable for Molly's business.

"It is fibre glass lined with barn doors. It belonged to a baker chap who is retiring soon. It has fitted trays as well, needs a bit of work done but nothing that I cannot manage" explained Rob feeling pleased with himself.

Simon and Rob agreed to meet up sometime in the next few days and give the van a once over and if they thought it to be a fair price, they would put in an offer. Molly was excited.

"I've got lots of ideas for logos" she tells them "It's got to be something bold and colourful and with contact details of course."

"You could always ask Stuart for ideas. He is very artistic when it comes to sign writing" suggest Rob.

"That sounds like a great idea. I will give him a call later" says Molly. She looks across the room to the fireplace where both Al and Stuart are enjoying a pint of beer and chatting with friends. She catches Stuart's eye, and he smiles and raises his glass to her in response. Molly had always thought of Stuart as good looking. She had been surprised when he had come out and when he had told them that he and Alan were a couple and had been ever since they had met at college. No one could have been more surprised than Molly. At the time she had felt a little embarrassed. Not because she had felt it difficult to accept. On the contrary that was the easy bit. It was just her persistent flirting and teasing every time their paths had crossed when the subject of girlfriends had come up. Al and Stu did not bear any ill will and had remained good friends with everyone in Molly's circle.

Conversation was becoming more difficult. The background sounds of music and singing as well as the sound of laughter and cheering from within the crowded room had become deafening. Jenny was walking towards their table, smiling, and waving a piece of paper in her hand and again everyone cheered.

"Well done my lovely! She shouts to Molly in her familiar west country accent "you have won the third burning." Smiling she hands over the small envelope to Molly containing the prize money.

"Thanks Jenny, first time for me" she replied raising the envelope high so everyone could see her winnings, which set of another round of cheering.

Both Rob and Iris had won a prize at the previous year's burning.

"I think drinks are on you, shall I get them in?" Simon was already on his feet and was gathering the empty glasses from the table.

"Must make it my last one though, if we plan to go sale shopping tomorrow" said Molly to Iris.

"Same here!" Came the response. "I'm feeling a bit tiddly already, but I think I can manage just one more for the road."

With their replenished drinks the four friends, now unable to make themselves heard because of the noise, joined in with the singing of the choruses of songs they knew. A medley of songs from the old music halls echoed around the room. Those not wanting to sing were clapping along instead. The hubbub sounds of banter and laughter intertwining with the singing.

"Come on Molly" came a shout from someone across the room. "This is your song. Come and sing with us."

Molly knew there was no way she would get out of this and in a strange way she quite enjoyed being appreciated for her ability to at least be able to sing in tune.

Shouts of pleading from around the room and table banging noise turned into whistles and applause as she got to her feet. All her inhibitions gone due to the amount of wine she had consumed and with encouragement from her own table, Molly pushed forward to where the band were set up.

People at the back began to stand on their chairs not wanting to miss the chance of seeing Molly's performance. With the guitar chords strummed, she started to sing her favourite song.

ONCE UPON A TIME THERE WAS A TAVERN, WHERE WE USE TO RAISE A GLASS OR TWO....

Encouraging everyone to join in with the chorus Molly sang through the microphone as the music began to speed up. Her audience stood up and joined in willingly. When her song finished, she enjoyed a rapturous applause before taking her leave ignoring calls for an encore. The musicians continued with their repertoire.

"Well done, Mol" said Gary patting her on her back as she fought her way back to her table. "That was great."

Molly had a sudden flashback remembering Gary Thompson in her dream.

"Thanks Gary" she replies relieved he could not see her red face.

Returning to her table Iris hugged her friend with great enthusiasm.

"Didn't feel like taking your clothes off then." She spoke mischievously into Molly's ear not wanting their partners to hear.

"What was that you said?" Rob had heard the not so quiet question and was intrigued.

"Private girl talk" came the reply in unison as they both fell about in fits of laughter.

"Oh, Iris don't make me laugh, it's a good job I'm wearing my discrete Tena knickers."

A Snowy Valentine

Chapter 1

With the festivities now behind them it was time for Molly and Iris to turn their thoughts to business and productivity.

Everything was working out just as they had planned. Both Molly and Iris had spent a full week cleaning and restocking the kitchen. They had left the cleaning of the two large ovens till last and they proved to be the most challenging of appliances to clean. Molly had got up early to apply the caustic cleaning solution well before Iris arrived. The lengthy instructions had read that for best results the oily smelly goo was best left on for a minimum of two hours to allow it to infiltrate the excessive covering of splattered ground-in grease.

With just under an hour still to wait Molly chose two of the now eleven new hen painted mugs from the cupboard and proceeded to make each a coffee. Iris was quick to notice that the set of what was originally four hen design china mugs, and had become three following the breakage of one, had now multiplied filling Molly's allotted cupboard space. Iris had been unable to purchase a single mug so had decided to buy a complete set of four to replace the broken one. And as the price had been dramatically reduced in the sale, she had bought another set for herself.

"Oh Molly, so many mugs!" she exclaimed, concerned that she had over done it.

"Been meaning to tell you Iris! On the same day you gave me another set, which I might add, you really should not have, Si bought a set, also in the sale as he was feeling guilty for breaking one in the first instance."

Iris found this very amusing and started to laugh.

"At least when Si breaks another" her emphasis on the word when as opposed to if. "Then I shan't have to worry about it" said Molly light-heartedly.

From her carrier bag Iris took out a round tin containing one of her special coffee and walnut layered cakes. Molly's eyes widened and she began to salivate.

"Wow! Iris that looks amazing. When did you find time to bake that?"

"Late last night when I could not sleep. Think we deserve this after all the challenging work this week" she exclaimed cutting two thick slices.

"And why were you not able to sleep? Did I not work you hard enough yesterday?" Molly teased.

"I am just so excited about the baking, and I keep getting new ideas. I need to keep getting out of bed to jot them down before I forget" she relied.

"Oh! Iris how would I manage without your enthusiasm and ideas," said Molly. "You really do have a flair for this sort of thing" she said causing Iris to blush embarrassingly, and Molly gave her a hug.

Two mugs of coffee later and having both eaten and enjoyed a large slice of the irresistible moist coffee cake that Iris had brought with her that morning, they both set to work on the ovens.

"Give you a race Mol" Iris challenged, putting on a pair of rubber gloves and throwing a second pair to Molly.

"You're on!"

The caustic cleaning goo had worked wonders and in less than the recommended two hours making the cleaning easier than it might have been otherwise. Both ovens were soon near to being spotless.

"I think we deserve another piece of that delicious cake" said Molly, smiling at her friend, while at the same time looking for an excuse to have yet another mug of coffee.

"Phew! I'm having a bit of a hot flush, better make mine tea this time. I am trying to cut down on my coffee intake" said Iris, taking out a packet of tissues from her handbag. Removing one she began wiping away the beads of sweat that had accumulated across her forehead.

"I seem to be having a lot more hot flushes and the night sweats are getting worse too."

Looking at her friend, Molly could see that Iris was indeed extremely uncomfortable and that her face had turned a puce colour. The winter sun was shining directly into the room through the long length of the glazed window. Molly opened a top window and drew down a blind to block out the sun.

"I'm considering taking HRT" Iris blurted out, taking her friend completely by surprise "Or I should say I'm thinking about it."

This was not like Iris at all. Iris had made it quite clear to Molly that she was determined to get through her menopause using only natural remedies. Molly up till now had kept to herself the fact that she was considering doing the same, for fear of being persuaded to try yet another of Iris's herbal cures. Now they were both in agreement.

"Can I ask you something personal Mol? she asked, not waiting for a reply before adding: "Do you have any problem with sex?"

By now as was often the case when the pair had got together, they both started to giggle.

"I was not enjoying it as much as I use to, if I'm honest" she answered, with a broad grin, before continuing.

"Had a bit of dryness down below until I discovered this amazing lubricant" Molly added opening a drawer and taking out a large tube of ointment to show Iris.

"Wow! Mol, how much lubricant do you need? Or should I ask how many times do you have it?

Their giggles progressed to a more hysterical form of laughter.

"Don't make me laugh Iris, I might wet myself" Molly said crossing her legs and jigging about. Accepting one of Iris's tissues to dry her moist eyes.

"Being serious though Iris! I have been giving some thought to using HRT as well. Sometimes I feel so miserable I just don't know how to cope. I was only discussing it with Si last night" said Molly as she turned her attention to filling the kettle.

"I have tried everything too! Iris replied "It's such a bummer! As you know, I hate taking prescription medicine for anything. I'm so awful to Rob sometimes. It's a wonder he does not leave me" said Iris knowing full well that Rob would never do that.

Molly turned her attention to making them both a second hot drink.

She thought about joining Iris in having tea but decided against it.

Iris opened the cake tin and cut two more large slices of cake, placing a slice on each of their plates before sitting herself down on one of the three low back high stools next to the work bench. Being of a shorter stature than her friend, Iris had sometimes found it difficult getting herself up on the stools and it usually took more than one attempt. Once in position she had found them to be comfortable to sit on. Molly had chosen them, taking into consideration that they would both be sitting for lengthy periods of time when working at the bench.

"This is so greedy but lovely! You make the best coffee and walnut cake ever Iris."

"It's all right for you Mol, you never seem to put on any weight. I only need to look at cake and the pounds go on."

It was true. Molly could stuff herself with all sorts of high calorific foods and still her weight never seemed to change.

"Guess I'm lucky, I've got a naturally high metabolism!"

"And a naturally high libido, if the size of that tube is anything to go by" stated Iris setting off the pair of them to start giggling again.

… … … … …

With just a couple of days before baking would commence, orders were continuing to come in. Far more than they had anticipated.

The new van was also ready. Rob had sprayed the body in a dazzling, bright pink colour and Stuart had decorated it with a colourful array of assorted cupcakes. The bold inscription written on both sides of the van advertising their produce and contact phone numbers and emails stood out. Stuart had done a fantastic job.

Simon with help from Rob had scrupulously scrubbed it out and varnished the trays with a waterproof lacquer. They fixed boxes to the right inside door to carry rolls of lining paper. To the left side door, they fitted similar with secure pockets of assorted sizes. These Molly and Iris were able to fill with domestic utensils, writing material and any useful things that they thought they might need.

Molly and Iris cleaned and prepared the kitchen methodically. Everything was ready to go.

Chapter 2

The following day was to be a well-earned day off. Molly had made plans to meet her friend in town for coffee so they could discuss the ideas that Iris had for new decorations. She also had to collect some more specialised ingredients and flavourings from her supplier in town. These were the ones that Connor the store holder had not kept in stock and had to order in especially and were now ready for collection.

Molly had driven (Rosie) the name she had given the van, several times and after a hiccup or two, had become confident with its idiosyncrasies. The five-mile short journey into town was an easy one and she had driven it frequently. Parking the van was also not difficult due to the car's small size.

Getting out of Rosie, Molly hurriedly put on her coat, pulling up her collar as she did so. Glancing up at the sky she noticed the cloud formation beginning to change. It was looking a bit ominous, and she knew she would have to keep an eye on the weather. From the pocket of the door, she took out her hat and gloves and put them on, all the while shivering. From the glove box she retrieved the small purse containing assorted coins, that she had placed in the vehicle to pay for any parking. She knew exactly where the parking machine was located and headed towards it. The chilly wind was blowing in from the east and a weather warning had been given out by the presenter on the radio earlier that day for possible light snow showers. It was only after the third attempt to put the coins into the machine did Molly realise it was not working.

"Dam and blast" she said aloud and then glanced behind to see if anyone was watching her. Deciding that she would take a chance and that it was not her fault that the machine was not working she hastily made her way back to the car. Removing her gloves, she speedily wrote an apologetic but blunt note to leave on the windscreen of her car. By now she was not only cold but becoming irritable and it was close to coffee time! Molly never liked being late for anything especially when a cup of coffee was involved.

Locking the door, Molly scanned the car park for Iris's car but could not see it. The coffee shop that was to be their meeting place was situated in the arcade off the main high street. Knowing she was running late for her meeting with Iris, Molly quickened her pace counting three other coffee shops on her way. "Why hadn't I suggested one of those" she thought to herself, glancing in the windows and seeing others sitting at tables and already enjoying their beverages. This made her feel more irritable than ever. Turning a corner off the high street she could see the coffee shop just three doors down. Once inside the door Molly spied her friend sitting at a table and was relieved to see her and noticed she was already enjoying a hot drink.

"Sorry I am late. It has not been a good day so far. The ticket machine wasn't working in the car park" Molly moaned as she removed her gloves and coat that she had worn to protect her from the outside elements. Iris, as was the custom when they met together, gave Molly a quick hug.

"Not to worry Mol, not been here very long myself" she replied waving the tube of lubricant that she had just purchased from the chemist, causing them both to giggle.

The waiter came over and took Molly's order and within a few minutes she too was enjoying the large black coffee that she so desperately needed.

"That feels better" she said as she took her first mouthful of the steamy hot liquid.

Iris took out a large notepad from her handbag and excitedly began to show Molly the designs she had drawn.

"Iris, these are amazing. You are so talented, they are beautiful."

Happy with the positive reaction, Iris's face beamed.

"I'm so glad that you like them, I'm especially pleased with the valentine ones, and I can't wait to see how they will turn out."

"I took another order yesterday, so we now have twelve dozen valentine cupcakes to make as well as a few smaller orders spread throughout the rest of the month" Molly told Iris.

"That's great news Mol" Iris replied with enthusiasm.

"Just hope I haven't overstretched us both" said Molly looking to her friend for any signs of disapproval.

"I'm really looking forward to getting going again and I know it's going to be a good year" Iris said confidently, raising her cup as if to make a toast and to which Molly joined in and raised hers before downing the last mouthful.

"Shall we have another coffee and a sandwich to celebrate" Molly suggested looking at her watch and all the while thinking she should be getting home.

"Good idea" Iris said in total agreement.

The half hour prearranged coffee meeting turned into a one-and-a-half-hour lunch break. This was not unusual for the couple. Having consumed their sandwiches followed by a slice of cake each and a further two more cups of coffee, it was Molly who, looking at her watch, decided it was time to make a move. She still had shopping to do and wanted to get home before it snowed.

Because the coffee shop was in the arcade, neither of them were prepared for the extent of snow that had already fallen and was covering the ground and continuing to fall outside.

"Oh! blast, didn't expect this Mol" Iris said pulling up the collar of her coat, shivering once again.

"Me neither" Molly replied putting on her gloves and smiling to herself.

"I do like to see the snow but preferably from a window at home."

Turning to her friend, Iris gave the customary quick hug and kiss on her cheek.

"Didn't notice your car in the car park!" Molly said, having now assumed that Iris had taken a bus instead of driving herself into town.

"Can I give you a lift home? Just got to pick up a package from Salisbury's then I am heading straight home before it gets any worse," said Molly.

"Thanks that would be great if you don't mind" replied Iris, who was becoming concerned that the bus may not be running in this weather.

"I really didn't expect the snow till much later" said Iris to her friend.

Both women agreed that the weather forecaster had got it wrong again. Linking arms, as they often would, they set off down the high street.

It was a short diversion to Salisbury's to collect Molly's order. As they reached the shop door Connor, who saw her approaching, was eagerly waiting for Molly with a package in his hand.

"Wasn't sure if you were going to make it in this weather!" he said to Molly, handing over the order she had been waiting for. Connor was feeling anxious because of the sudden change in the weather. He had already phoned his wife Julie to say he would be shutting up early and heading straight home soon. He knew she would be worrying about him.

"Sorry Connor I'm afraid we got chatting and forgot the time" said Molly, taking the package from him and giving him a kiss on the cheek in return. "Thank you I'm so grateful that you stayed open for me, a lot of shops appear to be closing early."

Connor was quite use to Molly's friendly show of affection and quite enjoyed it. He always wished his wife Julie could be a little more like Molly and not so strait laced all the time.

"I knew the order was important to you so I wouldn't have closed until you got here" Connor replied before cheekily telling her how he looked forward to tasting her cupcakes again. The three of them exchanged good-humoured banter before the two women, once again linking their arms, set off and headed back to the car.

There was a light covering of snow across the car park. Molly did not have any difficulty spotting Rosie as she was the only vehicle left there. They hurriedly made their way to the car, occasionally having to support each other to prevent one or other from slipping on the wet icy ground. Their giggly happy mood changed abruptly when they saw the fixed charge penalty notice stuck to the windscreen. Molly had totally forgotten about the broken or empty payment machine. On the ground she saw the now wet and soiled note that she had written in haste and had placed on the screen just a couple of hours ago.

"Would you believe it!" she said before explaining to Iris how this had happened. "I don't intend to pay the fine though, I shall fight it just like I did the last two I had, after all it's not my fault if the bloody machine isn't working."

"If you need a witness Mol you've' got one" said Iris squeezing Molly's gloved hand reassuringly.

"Thanks Iris I know I can always rely on you," said Molly.

"However I know Carl Garland at the council offices quite well now, I will just take him a couple of my larger cupcakes like I did last time. He will do anything for them." Molly grinned and winked at Iris whose serious face changed to one of amusement and she began to chuckle.

"Oh! Mol you are a terrible flirt."

It was to be a slow drive home. The snow was beginning to fall more heavily. Molly had to concentrate harder on her driving. She was concerned that Rosie might not be up to it. With encouraging words from them both she behaved herself magnificently and got them safely home.

"Thanks for the lift Mol" Iris said before patting the dashboard of the car and thanking Rosie as well.

"I think we have a good one here in our Rosie" she says.

"Thanks to your Rob" Molly replied smiling to her friend.

"See you tomorrow."

Chapter 3

Baking day was now upon them. Both Molly and Iris were excited and keen to get going. With snow on the ground outside and the ovens warming up it meant that the kitchen was a very welcoming place to be in. With the plentiful supply of basic cupcake ingredients Molly set to adding butter and sugar to the large mixer that had stood idle for the last few weeks.

The whirring sound of the mixing machine at first seemed quite normal especially considering that it had not been in use for a while. Molly cracked open the bowl of eggs on the work top examining them in preparation for adding to the mix. With the creaming almost complete and the eggs ready to add came a different not so healthy sound from the food mixer. The motor became louder and began making grinding sounds. Molly turned in time to see small pieces of creamed fat and sugar being expelled high into the air. The machine then promptly accelerated to such a speed forcing even more of its contents out of the bowl covering everything around it. The newly clean work surfaces and walls behind them were a mess.

Molly rushed to turn off the machine, and she too became splattered with the mixture. Globules of wet fat stuck in her hair and clothes alike. The machine gave out a loud explosive bang finally bringing the mixer to a standstill, and this immediately was followed by bellowing puffs of smoke from the whisk attachment. It had died but not before having thrown out the entire contents of the bowl. At arm's length Molly quickly turned off the electric socket at the wall.

"Oh! Bloody hell! I don't believe it" she said crossly, standing a little away from the counter as she took in the devastation that surrounded them. The machine was knackered. The office a mess.

It was that final bang that had brought Iris to her feet and made her give out a piercing scream. She had been sitting on her stool mixing colour to sugar. In her haste to help Molly she jumped from her stool. Turning around her elbow came in to contact with three of the unstable bags of brightly coloured icing sugar and Iris accidentally knocked them all onto the floor. The powdered sugar was expelled into the air. Before it made landfall onto the floor it showered them both as well as covering worktops and implements alike. "Sorry! Sorry! Sorry …," shouted Iris.

From another part of the house came running in Simon who had heard the commotion. Entering 'Molly's office' he was faced with what looked like a slapstick comedy and on seeing that the ladies were safe started laughing. Both the women were standing as if in shock, splattered with cake mix and coloured icing sugar. What had been a clean working environment had become an absolute mess.

"Don't you dare laugh" Molly shouted to Simon having recovered from the initial shock. "How are we ever going to get the cakes made in time for tomorrow" she continued with a raised voice while at the same time becoming extremely anxious causing beads of perspiration to run down her face.

Wiping her face with her hand only made her appear even more hilarious.

"It's ok Mol don't fret so, we'll get it sorted" Simon said reassuringly turning to Iris and looking for her support.

"Of course, we will Mol" Iris added having caught the eye of Simon, who by now just wanted to laugh at the situation.

Molly began to feel a hot flush coming on again. She started clenching her fists and her body started shaking. Picking up the soiled tea towel from the table she began fanning herself and moved quickly to the window. Opening it to take in the cool breeze, was she knew the quickest way to relieve the uncomfortable and awful feelings. Having taken a few deep breaths, Molly was able to more calmly take in the fulness of the situation that now lay before her in the room. Looking down and taking in her own appearance and then glancing across at Iris, who she thought was looking almost ghostly, she began to giggle. Iris, who had been biting her bottom lip and stifling a giggle herself, began to relax and it was not long before they both began to laugh.

Shortly afterwards and taking charge of the situation as she knew she could, Iris suggested that they should start by cleaning themselves up and then put the kettle on before they tackle the clean-up operation. Simon offered to buy Molly a new mixer the following day but that would not help the dilemma she was in now.

It was a practical Iris that came up with the suggestion that if she helped to make the cakes as well as Molly and using an old- fashioned hand-method they could still complete the orders in time.

"What would I do without you?" Molly was even more grateful for her partner's sensible and practical approach.

"That's what being best friends is all about" she replied. "And I'm sure we can rope in Si and Rob to help with the creaming too."

Much later that afternoon with the clearing up done the two women gathered what they needed from the cupboards. With their overly large combination of metal and plastic bowls and a selection of wooden spoons and with the help of the two men they were ready to cream the butter and sugar together beating in the eggs before folding in flour and lastly adding Molly's special essence of flavours. Molly then placed the loaded baking trays into the hot ovens.

They all patiently waited, both feeling a little apprehensive to see whether the cakes would rise as well as they usually had, when they had made them by machine. They were not to be disappointed as the cakes turned out perfectly. Each cake lightly brown in colour and with a distinctive smell were ready to be transferred to cooling racks.

It now only left the making of an array of flavoured butter creams. Molly accurately measured the ingredients into seven individual bowls. She then carefully placed labels next to these denoting which colourings and flavouring she planned to add to each mix.

It was fortunate that Iris had been planning and making the most exquisite sugar decorations through the month of January. There were tiny red roses entwined with hearts for the valentine orders as well as other assorted ones which had been specific orders for individual customers. Molly was delighted.

"These are amazing Iris!" said Molly as her eyes spanned the intricately worked sugar pieces.

"Thanks! Mol, I have had such fun making them" she said, delighted that her friend had approved.

"Rob is so clever making these moulds as well" said Molly who was examining and admiring the small plastic pieces, shaped and cut to size.

"Wait till you see the ones he is working on now!" Iris proudly replied.

By the time, the butter creams were ready the cakes had cooled. Sitting side by side they set to and iced the cakes and then added the final toppings. All that remained to do was to box each batch ready for delivery the following day and of course the cleaning up.

What had started out to be an eventful day when it looked like everything was going wrong had ended well. Through the window they could see the sky was beginning to darken. No more snow had fallen for which they were grateful. Gathering her things together, Iris made ready to leave.

"Fancy a glass of wine before you go?" offered Molly knowing opening a bottle was the first thing she was going to do.

"Why not" Iris replied placing her things back down on the table.

"I think we both deserve it!"

Switching off the lights and securing the door behind them, Molly and Iris walked the few steps to Molly's own kitchen leaving the warmth and smell of fresh baking behind them. Unlike the minimalistic working office which naturally needed to be practical, functional, and kept scrupulously clean, this room felt cosier and more welcoming. Molly's worktops and shelves were all cluttered with an assortment of ornaments and utensils. Scribbled paper notes were stuck to more than one of the cupboard doors. Cookery books were stacked high on top of the units. Some books were in neat piles and appeared to be new, while others were left open with torn covers and dogeared corners. Some of these containing many of Molly's favourite and most frequently used recipes. On the odd occasion when Simon had tried to tidy the books away it had caused a row between them so now, he just leaves them until Molly herself decides to have a tidy up.

"What was the use of tidying then away just to get them down again from the top shelf?" she would argue.

Rob, having helped with the creaming had returned home. He had just come back to walk Iris home so was already enjoying a glass of wine while chatting and laughing with Simon. Molly supposed that the men had been discussing the earlier event which had taken place in the office. The abrupt ceasing of laughter and chatter culminating with the guilty look they both showed on their faces was a giveaway. As the women approached it was a relief to the men to see they were both smiling. The calamity of the afternoon put behind them. Without hesitation Simon took out two more glasses from the cupboard and without offering he poured two large glasses of wine.

"Here you go you two, think you both deserve this after today" said Simon, pulling out chairs for them to sit down.

"You poor things" Rob added trying to sound serious.

Rob was still finding it difficult not to laugh but he knew that he had to appear more sombre for fear of upsetting Molly.

Having drunk their first glass of wine and it was only when they were on their second that the women began to relax and enjoy the men's banter.

"I hope you're not finding it funny Rob" said a serious Iris, looking into her husband's face for any tell-tale signs. "Because it really wasn't, at least not at the time" she said.

Feeling a little sorry for Rob, Molly hastily responded explaining that they must put it in the past and move on. Smiling she raised her glass and proposed a toast to the team.

"I think we could cope with anything that Molly's cupcake business throws at us after today" replied Iris. With this the four friends shared the remains of the wine bottle and Simon went for another one to open.

"By the way Mol, your new mixer should be delivered tomorrow. You can call it a Valentines gift from me."

"That's fantastic Si" replied a more relaxed Molly.

"And you can have two of the larger cupcakes you helped to make today for your valentine gift!" she smiled licking her top lip seductively.

Chapter 4

The following morning Molly got up early to prepare for the deliveries that she needed to make that day. Simon was still sleeping, that is until she planted a light kiss on his lips and wished him a happy Valentine's Day.

"You're not getting up, yet Mol are you? It's far too early and I want a cuddle" he responded, grabbing her arm with one hand, and pulling back the duvet with the other trying to entice her back to bed.

"You must have time for a quickie."

"No time for any of that this morning" she teasingly replied offering her lips for a more lingering kiss. She too would have rather got back into bed and cuddle up to his warm body, but needs must, and she knew this was an important day.

"I will make some coffee and bring you a cup up. There is no need for you to get up yet."

It was still dark outside. Molly quickly showered and dressed. Applying a light moisturiser to her face and running a comb through her hair was all the time she could allow herself this morning. As she went downstairs it was still necessary to put on more lights. The kitchen was warm. With the kettle on Molly went to pull up the blinds to see the first signs of dawn.

"Oh! Bloody hell" she shouted.

Simon had been hoping for a lie in. Molly's refusal to stay in bed had disappointed him. He did not need to go into college early as he had no lectures planned for the morning so was looking forward to not getting up for his usual time. Fully awake and sitting up in bed Simon waited for his coffee. He thought when Molly came back, he might be able to try his luck with her again. Simon reached for his phone which he kept on his bedside table. This was something he did religiously every morning. He was just checking his hundred and one emails at least that is what it seemed like every morning when he turned his phone on when he heard Molly shout.

"What is it my love. Is everything ok?" he shouted back.

"Look out the window" Molly shouted in response.

Simon replaced his phone and got out of bed to do as Molly had suggested.

Heavy snow was falling, and it looked like it had been snowing throughout the night for the amount that lay on the ground.

Putting on his dressing gown and grabbing his phone Simon joined Molly in the kitchen.

"There's nothing on my phone to suggest we were in for all this snow" he said, swiping his pages to check the weather forecast.

"Oh, for goodness' sake Si! Your dam phone. What am I going to do. How am I going to do the deliveries today?"

Simon put down his phone. He knew how Molly felt about him always checking it.

"I'm sure the roads will be cleared by the time you have loaded the van."

The snow indeed looked very deep outside. It was difficult to see the chicken runs at the bottom of the garden.

The whole area was deep in snow. He was almost sure though, that the chickens would be safely snuggled together inside their hutches.

Molly knew she could not think clearly until she had had her morning coffee. Hurriedly Simon went back upstairs to dress, muttering how she was not to worry, and that he would help her. Molly made the coffee and poured each of them a steaming mug full.

Simon returned dressed but unshaved. Picking up his mug he sipped the hot coffee. Side by side the pair of them stood staring out of the window. Simon put his arm around Molly's shoulders as she let out a significant sigh of disappointment.

"What am I going to do? All those cakes!"

"Don't worry we'll think of something." Simon could see that Molly was close to tears. "Pour me another coffee love while I have a think!"

Simon continued staring out of the window willing the snowfall to stop. After just a few more frustrating minutes watching the skies, the falling snow was beginning to ease, and the dark clouds were drifting away. The morning light making visibility clearer. The damage however had been done.

Simon put on his wellies and overcoat and went outside to assess the situation. Opening the back door, he could not distinguish where the footpath and the garden area met. To his right he saw the garage door knowing his own car was safely inside. However, outside he could see the shape of another vehicle covered in thick snow that he knew to be that of Rosie. There was no way, he thought to himself, that Rosie was going anywhere today.

Rob and Iris who only lived a couple of houses down from them were trudging up towards the house. Dressed for the arctic in their winter coats and identical woolly bobble hats, gloves, and scarves that their daughter had knitted them for Christmas. Both were wearing green wellington boots. It was a sight to make anyone smile. Even on this disastrous day.

Looking out the window Molly saw that the pair were approximately two feet off to where the path would have been under the snow, and she could not help but smile to herself. As they reached the door Molly was there to open it. Iris hugged her.

They were both devastated especially after all the arduous work they had put in the day before to ensure that every customer would get their orders on time. Neither of them had any ideas as to what they were going to do.

The four of them were now together in Molly's warm kitchen. It was still early.

"I think we should have breakfast" suggested Simon. "Scrambled eggs alright for everyone?"

"Thanks Si that would be great. We haven't had anything other than a quick cup of tea," said Rob.

"Could not believe our eyes when we looked out the window could we Rob? said Iris.

Rob offered to make toast while Molly made fresh coffee.

"If it is any help, I am not planning to go into work today. Not sure I could get there any way," said Rob. He had phoned his two employees, waking them both up and informing them not to travel out and that he would keep the garage workshop closed for the day.

Simon thought it unlikely that the college would be open any time that day but just needed to phone in to check.

Sitting around the kitchen table all four tucked into a breakfast of scrambled eggs and bacon followed by stacks of thick brown toast and Molly's homemade marmalade. All had decided to have coffee.

Discussing the inclement weather where each joked of their own memories and experiences on past similar situations was fun for a short while. It was Iris who noticed that Molly kept looking towards the window where significant more daylight was now apparent.

"Any ideas anyone how we can deliver the cakes today?" she asked turning the conversation to a more serious one.

It would once again be Rob who would come to the rescue, albeit with a bizarre idea.

"There's definitely no way we will be able to get our cars out today and having made a phone call earlier to a mate I know the road is partially blocked too" he said.

"Well, that's helpful isn't it my dear!" said Iris interrupting him.

"Let me finish love!" he said to Iris before continuing. "We often walk into the village, don't we?" and they all agree listening to him and wondering what he could be planning.

"You know the old barrow at the bottom of our garden!" he said having now got Iris's attention.

"The barrow you insisted I did up so you could loan it to the fete committee last year" he was teasing Iris.

"Between us, I think we could pull it through the snow. The wheels are thick, and I might add in good nick!" he added, feeling quite pleased with himself making everyone smile at his attempt to lighten the mood.

Molly, who had initially thought it had been a preposterous proposal, began to warm to Rob's idea. So far no one else could produce any alternative suggestions so after blunt discussion and deliberation they then started to work out how they could secure the boxes of cakes securely to the barrow. Once again it was Rob who came to the rescue.

"We can use the shelves from Rosie, I'm sure I can fix them, so they won't move."

"There is one large order for the bakery" Molly said as she was thinking aloud "and five smaller boxes to be delivered to addresses in the village."

Within the next hour Simon and Rob, having dug out the old, what was once an old market stall, had pulled it out of the snow to Molly's back door. They unbolted the trays from the van and set to securing them onto the barrow. Meanwhile the two women secured the cake boxes into the deeper lipped baker's trays that they had planned to use in Rosie. Within a brief time and only after playful squabbles where everyone thought they may have a better idea than the other where to clear a pathway to the road were they ready to go.

"What must we look like?" Molly says to Iris as they both started to giggle. Dressed warmly in thick coats and colourful accessories and all wearing wellington boots, they set off.

Neighbours' curtains were twitching as they watched from their windows after hearing the commotion outside. The sounds of elated banter dispersed with the sound of the squeaky barrow made such a scene.

"Eh Iris look over there!" says Molly tilting her head on one side to show in which direction Iris should look.

"Nosey cow!" she says as she is just in time to see PP withdrawing back behind her nets. "Doesn't miss a thing does she, I wonder what she will make of all this."

"Do you know something Iris? I just don't give a hoot."

Prudence and Michael Edwards lived on the opposite side of the street to Molly and Iris. Pru as she was known was very prudish in her manner at about everything, hence the nickname PP for Prudish Pru they had given her behind her back. When the couple had first moved into the street Molly and Iris had gone out of their way to make them feel welcome and part of their social group. Pru however, they had quickly discovered had no sense of humour and when the pair had dressed up on Halloween and had knocked on their door shouting trick or treat, Pru however had not been amused. She told them in no uncertainty that they were behaving childishly.

In contrast their partners had got on well with Michael, even inviting him for a round of golf. So, it was for Michael's sake that Molly and Iris persevered with their friendship towards Pru. It was difficult. So, behind her back they continued to refer to her as PP.

The men continued to pull the cart while the women at the rear pushed. They followed along the tyre tracks that had been left by a lone passing truck that had driven by sometime before them. For this they had been grateful. Stopping occasionally, just to clean off impacted snow from the wheels and checking that the load was secure, the procession steadily progressed the one and a half miles into the village.

The first delivery was to the bakers. Inside the baker was relieved to see Molly as he had been concerned that he would not get the valentine specials that he had ordered and had advertised for his customers.

By now there were more onlookers as people started to venture out of their houses to see the snow. Typically, and not unexpectedly there came jeers and laughter from people they had known. They knew that this escapade would be gossiped or joked about for a long time to come.

Deliveries were made to two coffee shops. One at each end of the street. The remaining boxes of cakes being distributed to private houses with the last one for the sewing shop, where Beverley worked and was planning to celebrate her fiftieth birthday.

With clear skies the sun began to give out welcoming warmth and the snow was becoming more like slush. Their job was completed and the weary four headed for home.

The return journey was less harrowing due to the now empty barrow and everyone's jubilant feeling of finally completing the last successful delivery. Molly and Iris could relax thanks to Rob's ingenious idea and both partners' strength.

With the two men pulling the cart and in deep conversation about their disappointment of not being able to play golf that day, the women took turns to jump on the back of the cart for an easier ride home all the while trying not to laugh to loudly so as not to be caught.

"Happy Valentine's Day" Simon, suddenly shouted out taking them both by surprise when the men realised that both women were sitting on the back of the cart. The men released their grip on the wooden handles to tip both women off and into the snow.

"Serves you right the pair of you, I thought it was getting harder to pull" he says.

"This is one Valentine's Day I think none of us will ever forget" says Rob jovially as the two women get to their feet. Both were laughing loudly at the same time as complaining of their partner's prank. Getting up off the ground and in good humour Molly and Iris stop to brush off the snow before resuming their part in pushing the barrow the rest of the way home.

Later that evening the four gathered at Iris and Rob's house for a planned supper. Iris had made her delicious lasagne. As suggested Molly planned to contribute with a desert.

On seeing Molly standing at the door carrying a tray of left over cupcakes, they all fell about laughing. Instead of making a desert she had bought along the leftover cakes that had been destined for a delivery outside of the village which they were unable to get to.

"Well, I couldn't let them go to waste, could I!"

Chapter 5

Simon had been as good as his word and had bought Molly an even more superior catering size mixer to replace the one that had exploded.

The weather had improved. The remaining baking days of the last weeks had gone well, and every order safely delivered in Rosie.

Everyone in and around the village had got to recognise the pretty pink van decorated with colourful cupcakes. Even small children, some walking while others were being pushed along in their buggies, would wave to Molly and Iris as they drove past. Sometimes they would engage with them by tooting Rosie's horn, and this especially pleased the little ones.

Today was a non-baking day so Molly was using the time to catch up on her paperwork. Her office now included a small desk situated in the corner of the room. To the side of the desk Molly had added a tall filing cupboard where she kept all the documents relating to the business neatly in appropriate folders. On the desk was an extension phone off the main line to the house. This meant she could take orders from anywhere in the house. When Rob had been home, he knew he only needed to answer the phone after he had let it ring four times. He would then know he would not have to leave what he had been doing to find Molly. Mostly he would use his mobile phone for personal calls. The system was working well.

It was a sunny early spring morning and Molly was just going through her diary when the phone rang.

"Hello Molly, it's Pru here" came the voice from the other end. "Just wondering if you and Simon would like to come for drinks on Saturday. It is Michaels's birthday, and I know he would like Simon to help him celebrate."

A surprised Molly thought to herself that PP had not really wanted her to go but that she could not invite one without the other.

"I have invited Iris and Robert as well" she said hearing the pause at the other end of the line.

Why could she not bring herself to shorten their names like their other friends had, Molly thought to herself as she thought to respond.

"That's kind of you Prudence we would love to" she replied emphasising the word WE and using her full name knowing that she had preferred people to call her Pru.

"Lovely, shall we say seven thirty Molly and don't worry about supper as I will be serving a light buffet."

"We shall look forward to it" said Molly hoping, at the same time, Iris and Rob could make it.

… … …

At precisely seven thirty Molly and Simon crossed the road to Pru and Michael's house. This was only the second time that the four of them had been invited into their home.

In one hand Simon carried a bottle of whiskey in a greeting bag. As it was Michael's birthday celebration, and he knew how he had enjoyed a glass or two of whiskey after a round of golf, he thought this an appropriate gift. In his other hand he carried a bottle of wine.

Once inside Molly was relieved to see that Iris and Rob were already there enjoying a drink.

"Oh! What a coincidence" exclaimed Pru as Michael accepted his gift and took out the bottle of single malt whiskey. His face lit up.

"Thanks mate that's really kind of you" says Michael. "But you really shouldn't have."

Michael placed the bottle next to the one on the table that Rob and Iris had presented him with.

"Of course, Michael only enjoys an occasional whiskey and then only on special occasions" says Pru smiling at her husband.

It was obvious to everyone in the room apart from Pru, how much her husband really and frequently enjoyed his tipple.

Pru enjoyed entertaining. Since moving into the village, she and her husband had not yet made many acquaintances.

The few occasions when Pru had met both Molly and Iris she had not enjoyed their company, least of all their banter. She thought them both a silly pair.

Pru had been surprised to learn how popular both Molly and Iris were with everybody else. Both within the church congregation and the village itself and especially the pub. No one had anything but praise for them. She considered them to be of a status far below her normal network of social friends she had left behind in Kent.

However, their husbands were different, so she had thought. They seemed both friendly and polite. Conversing with them was easier. Pru thought them to be intelligent, especially Simon who she later found out was a lecturer at the college and that Robert owned his own business. They had quickly gone up in her initial estimate. Simon and Robert certainly were not silly like their wives.

It was important to Pru to help her husband find the right sort of friends. Individuals with a good standing. Well-mannered and cultured. She had already encouraged and baited her husband to offer his services to the church and the local council. It would not be long she thought before he would make a name for himself within their new community where they had made plans to settle into retirement. Golf had always been Michael's passion, and this is where he had met both Simon and Robert. It was, for his sake and the fact that they were neighbours, that she would make every effort to get on with their silly wives.

With large glasses of wine in their hand, Molly and Iris began to relax making polite conversation with their hosts. It was only when Pru left the room to check on food still in her oven did they discuss her snobbish behaviour.

"I'm sure, if she relaxed a little more, she could be quite nice" Molly said, surprised at her own comment.

"Perhaps we should get her tiddly and see if that would help" suggests Iris playfully giggling to her friend.

"More wine ladies!" said Michael, who had seen the empty glasses and was now walking towards them with a second bottle.

"Thank you" they both reply.

"Don't forget Pru's glass" says Iris seeing the half empty glass on the table where Pru had placed it before going to check on food.

"I'm not sure she will want another. One glass is all she usually has" says Michael as the women are persuading him to top the glass up as it was a special occasion.

Pru entered the room carrying a large tray of assorted savoury foods. She wanted to make an impression on her guests. Everyone she had met had nothing but praise for her neighbour's cake baking skills. She also knew that this was an area with which she could not compete. However, her pastry making was a different story and something special. Pru's friends back in Kent had often commented on the light texture of her butter pastry. Something of which she was proud. Over the years she had tried out new recipes and produced her own choice of ingredients for both sweet and savoury pastry. The fillings which she would once buy from a shop were now hand made.

All what Pru had prepared for this evening, she had carefully chosen to boast and show off her culinary skills.

"Please help yourselves" she said giving them each one of her best Royal Doulton tea plates and large damask linen napkins. Each napkin had been pressed to perfection. Iris, who had been amused by this, caught Molly's eye, and winked at her.

Molly and Iris watched as Pru picked up her glass of wine from the table. For a split second she studied the contents before taking a sip.

Dismissing the idea that Michael had topped up her glass she continued sipping her drink while making conversation within the group. Pru began to relax. Chatting had become easier, and she was warming to the females in the room.

By now the four guests who had been told not to eat dinner by their host because food would be served that evening were beginning to feel hungry. They started to tuck into the small meat and fish savouries as well as the sweet petit fours from the silver platters and other plates of food that had already been placed on the table earlier.

Michael was very attentive towards his guests, filling each of their glasses as soon as he noticed they were empty. He was surprised by his wife when she had requested a refill as well, noticing that her voice was becoming louder. To their surprise Molly and Iris found the food exceptionally tasty. The warm buttery pastries melting in their mouths.

"These are delicious" Molly says to Pru taking a second prawn filo pastry parcel from the plate that was being offered to her.

"You must let me have the recipe."

Iris did not wait to be offered anything. She felt brazen enough to help herself, filling her plate with a variety of pieces of food to try.

Much to Molly and Iris's surprise what they thought was going to be a posh and difficult evening, that neither of them had been looking forward to, was turning out to be quite pleasurable and fun. They were beginning to see Pru in a different light and were warming to her and her hospitality.

The men who had first consumed beer were now handed large glasses of whiskey. Michael had insisted he opened one of the two bottles his friends had bought him to try. A now very merry Pru did not seem to bat an eye lid.

"Can I offer any of you ladies a glass of whiskey?

They all declined but all three accepted the offer of yet another glass of wine. This time it was Pru who picked up a new bottle of wine to refill their glasses.

A sudden cry from Rob across the room made everyone look in his direction. Iris moved towards him. Not wanting to make a fuss, Rob apologised saying he had cramp in his leg and got up to walk around the room to ease the pain.

"Tonic water! That is what you need" said Pru. "I've got some in the kitchen" and she sped quickly across the room to the kitchen to get him some.

"Are you ok my love?" asks Iris. She noticed Rob surreptitiously take out a handkerchief from his trouser pocket bringing it to his mouth.

"Don't fuss dear I'm fine, really I am."

In truth Rob had bitten down on a small tartlet and had damaged a tooth. Spitting out what he thought was a piece of a broken tooth he managed to discretely place it in his trouser pocket. It was not long before he felt a sharp pain and took a large gulp of his whiskey. The last thing he wanted to do was to create any fuss or arouse Pru's suspicion and he was dreading having to down a glass of cold tonic water. More whiskey would be better he thought draining the remnants from his glass. He could only assume there had been a small foreign object in the pastry that he had just consumed.

Pru returned from the kitchen carrying a glass of cold fizzy tonic water. Politely Rob accepted. Pretending to rub his leg he winced as he drank the contents.

"Drink it all up now. It really will help I promise" says Pru watching as Rob empties the glass.

The pain in his mouth was excruciating. He accepted a generous top up of whiskey from Michael which he hoped would ease the throbbing ache in his mouth. He swallowed the warming amber liquid much quicker than he knew he ought in attempt to staunch the pain, but this was to no avail. A little whisper in Iris's ear saying that he was ready to go home bought the evening to its end.

They had stayed much longer than planned and had not expected to have enjoyed themselves so much. Michael collected their coats from the hallway helping the ladies on with their own.

Formalities completed both Molly and Iris displayed a moment of affection by kissing each of their hosts on the cheek.

"Thank you so much for coming. We are both so pleased you were able to help us celebrate Michael's birthday. Are we not dear?" said Pru reaching for her husband's hand and stroking it with her other. He smiled at her before turning to his guests and raised his eyebrows. It was obvious to him that Pru had drunk far more than she usually had.

"You know you do not have to leave yet. It is still early! We could open another bottle of wine" suggested Pru.

"Come on dear we must let our guests go home, busy day tomorrow" he said to the relief of their guests.

Closing the door behind them Pru who was more than a little merry praised her husband telling him how well she thought HER party had gone.

"I think we should host more evenings like this one. I think I might have been mistaken about Molly and Iris."

The four of them having crossed to the opposite side of the street and checking that their hosts had withdrawn inside their house; Rob was able to narrate the story about his broken tooth and how he did not want to upset Pru. He was confident that there had been something in a tartlet that he had eaten that should not have been there.

"Don't worry Rob your secret is safe with us," said a giggly Molly. Iris thought it was also very funny. She did not realise the pain Rob was in. The friends hugged each other before going their separate ways.

Two cups of coffee later and Molly and Simon went to bed. They both had felt a little drunk and the coffee had a sobering affect. Simon was in bed first hopeful that Molly might agree to sex. He recalled she had drunk more than a couple of glasses of wine, was a bit tipsy and did seem a bit flirty. However, this was not to be, not tonight it seemed.

Molly had noticed more often these days that her libido was not as evident as it used to be. Sometimes she had wanted to have sex and other times she most definitely did not, and this was one of them.

Molly had sometimes felt guilty. She knew that she would often tease Simon, especially when she had enjoyed a drink or two. Simon always tried to understand what his wife was going through with the menopause.

"I know you have tried to explain but can you tell me how long this menopause goes on for? I do sometimes feel it's going on a long time."

"Everyone is different," said Molly. "Some women go through it in months while others can take years."

"You are obviously going to be one of the long ones then" he said without thinking and realising once he had spoken that he sounded a bit sarcastic.

Molly burst into tears. The effects of the alcohol were beginning to wear off and she was tired. Simon felt guilty.

"Sorry love, I didn't mean it the way it sounded, I do really want to understand" he said, taking Molly into his arms and comforting her.

Molly loved Simon so much, she hated turning down his advances.

This was a time when she would relent and give in to him, albeit reluctantly. She knew he had needs and respected them. Sex was not as spontaneous or enjoyable as it was before the symptoms started. She longed for the time when she would feel more normal. Until then then she would just have to go through the motions and pretend.

Molly woke and looked at the clock. She had only been asleep for a couple of hours. She had woken with a feeling of stomach cramp and nausea. She felt hot and sweaty and very unwell. Pushing away the duvet she made a quick rush to the bathroom. Vomiting into the loo before urgently turning and lowering herself onto the seat just in time to pass diarrhoea splattering the pan. Staggering back towards the bedroom she was nearly knocked off her feet by Simon who rushed past her with the same urgency. Twice more during the night did Molly have the same churning feelings in her stomach and needed to vomit and had more diarrhoea. Simon however had to get to the bathroom on several more occasions. The pair groaned and moaned throughout the night. There was to be little sleep for either of them.

The alarm clock that had been set for 7am went off. Simon moved to cancel the irritating musical tune that was playing on his phone. He kept meaning to change the tune that was beginning to annoy him.

"Oh! my poor arse" he complained. "It feels like my insides have been torn out through my backside. Not sure I will be able to sit down for a week" he continued as he rolled from side-to-side moaning, trying to find a more comfortable position.

It was concerning to them both that something they had eaten the evening before had been the cause of their demise.

***

"Won't be able to play golf today" said Simon disappointedly. This being his first comment to Molly as she stirred from a restless night.

"Terrible shame!" Molly responded, not really fussed about it. She turned away pulling the duvet over her shoulders.

"Guess I better phone Rob to apologise and explain the situation" he said reluctantly getting out of bed to phone him.

"Good job it's Sunday and I don't have to get up" Molly said pulling back the duvet again that Simon had thrown off, leaving her to feel cold.

Molly decided to stay in bed but thought it would be most unlikely she would get any more sleep. She listened to the one-sided conversation as Simon was speaking with Rob. It did not take her long to realise that their friends had also had a rough night.

Returning to the bedroom Simon made to get back into bed.

"No point getting up yet if I cannot go and play golf, is there? Poor Rob not only did he have sickness and shits, but he also has a raging tooth ache to put up with."

Simon turned off the bedside lamp. The room was in semi darkness. It would be a brief time before both fell back to sleep. They both remained in bed for the rest of that morning.

***

Later that day Molly phoned Iris to check on her and Rob's condition and was pleased to find that like her and Simon they were feeling better, except that is for Rob's toothache.

"I managed to get an emergency appointment with the dentist for him tomorrow, until then I will just have to keep him dosed up" explained Iris.

"Cannot wait to tell PP we got food poisoning from her little party last night. I know she won't take it well" said Molly relishing the idea.

"I was going to stop calling her prudish Pru after last night. Once she relaxed and had at least three glasses of wine she was a much nicer person" said Iris "but now I won't because PP will stand for POISONER PRU" To which they both chuckled.

On reflection they had decided not to tell PP. They thought it would be too unkind.

"I wouldn't mind betting that they both suffered as well," said Molly.

"I bet they did; I hope she has a 'stegga' like I have" retorted Iris.

"A what!" Molly wanted to know, never having heard the expression before.

"You know," said Iris. "A steg-a- sore -Ars."

"Oh! Don't make me laugh Iris" said Molly as she started jigging around now desperate for a wee. "You'll make me wet myself!"

Chapter 6

Orders for Mothering Sunday cupcakes began to come in. Five small orders and three large bakery ones as well as other personal celebration party orders. Molly and Iris were excited to be busy, especially after the catastrophe of the valentine specials. Iris made her beautiful edible flowers as well as letters to make the word MUM in pink and yellow. She also made tiny green leaves to complement the individual flowers. As well as these Iris had also made beautiful colourful butterflies for a customer celebrating a special birthday. On a separate tray were tiny cricket bats, stumps and balls which had been requested by the wife of a member of the local cricket team for a surprise birthday party.

Molly had perfected just the right amount of cake mix, ensuring a perfectly risen cupcake and larger cakes every time.

Before boxing up the finished cakes Simon had decided that they ought to photograph them. He had suggested that they might one day create a pamphlet as a way of advertising their products.

Molly picked up two cakes holding one of each in front of her breasts. Seeing her friend doing this Iris followed suit.

"What do you think Simon?" Iris said chuckling and flaunting herself in front of him as he held his camera posed to take his first picture.

"Only if you are prepared to take of your clothes" he retorted back to the women who were dancing around in front of him.

"No! I don't think so. I think that's been done before" they both responded, simultaneously placing the cakes back on the table.

"Anyway, I don't think anyone would want to see my saggy boobs" Iris said cheekily.

"Me neither! said Molly.

Boxing up the cakes securely took time. The smaller special boxes for the individual orders were each wrapped in a ribbon before the labels were added. A number on each one was written to coincide with the order address.

The following day and with spring in the air an incredibly happy Molly and Iris loaded the van together. They set off in Rosie to make the deliveries. Driving through the villages stopping only to deliver their wares. By now Molly and Iris were quite used to people waving at them and other local vehicles hooting their horns as they passed them by.

The last delivery was made to Jane who was expecting them at precisely 10.30 when she knew her husband would be out. Jane was so pleased with how the cricket themed cake had turned out it bought tears to her eyes. She was so grateful to them both and hugged them in turn.

With the last delivery made Molly and Iris decided to stop at a coffee shop and partake of a cup of coffee and a slice of someone else's cake.

"Nowhere near as good as yours!" Iris said to Molly quietly, putting a second fork full of cake into her mouth and pulling a face.

"The sponge is a bit heavy" replies Molly pushing down on the cake with her finger before lifting a fork of cake to taste it. "Stodgy as well! That is probably why the layer of butter cream and jam is so thick" she said whispering to Iris, "Coffee is good though! Fancy another?"

Molly could never have just a single cup of coffee, it always had to be two. Iris however would sometimes decline especially if it were late in the day, but on this occasion she accepted.

"Need another one to wash down the gooey, sickly cake!" Iris replied, this time in not such a quiet voice and just as the waiter was walking past their table. Scowling at them she leant over to clear the crockery from the table.

"Can we get two more cups of coffee, please," asks Molly.

"Would you like more cake as well with that?" enquired the waiter sarcastically who was by now feeling bad tempered due to the criticism of her homemade cake.

"No thanks, just coffee" Molly and Iris replied at the same time.

When the waiter moved away from their table, they both started to giggle again causing her to turn her head in their direction. She had a face like thunder.

"Perhaps we better not come in here for a while" stated Iris who was beginning to feel a little guilty.

"Well, there are plenty of coffee shops to choose from and lots more cakes to try!" said Molly, downing the remaining cool dregs of coffee from her cup and wishing she could have yet another.

Rosie's
Day Out

Chapter 1

C hecking her calendar Molly saw that the celebration of Easter was going to be early this year. The spring weather was turning out to be more like early summer with warm sunshine and hardly any rain. Molly found herself taking an increasing number of orders for cupcakes. Both Iris and she were going to have a busy month ahead of them.

Sitting at her desk Molly was trying to plan the baking days necessary to complete the orders when the phone rang. It was Cheryl Goodfellow, one of the local primary school teachers. Molly recalled that she had made cakes for the school the year before.

"Hello, is that Molly's cupcakes? I'm not sure if you remember me but ...

"Yes of course I do Cheryl" Interrupted Molly priding herself on remembering all her customers. "How can I help you?"

"I appreciate I'm a little late, but I was hoping to order sixty Easter cupcakes for an end of term treat for classes one and two."

"I'm sure we can do that for you" said Molly, while at the same time thinking she may have been taking on too much. "Do you have any suggestions as to what decorations you would like?"

"Oh, thank you Molly. You are so kind. I am happy to leave the decorations to you. The children do so love your cupcakes and if you can let us have a little discount like last time, which would be much appreciated too" she says before dropping her next bombshell. "I know it's a lot to ask but I have another favour to ask you, we were wondering whether you and Iris would be our judges for the Easter bonnet parade?"

No matter how often Molly scolded herself for not thinking before she replied, she once again reluctantly agreed to do this and without consulting Iris.

Molly had always considered herself as not being 'particularly good' with young children, especially in large numbers. The last time she had faced a class of young ones was when she had agreed to do some baking with them. It had been last Christmas, just before term ended for the festivities and the children had been overly excited. The tableau of festive shaped biscuits that they had made had not turned out well. It was not so much that the biscuits themselves were the problem but the overly zealous nature of the little ones with the decorations. Never had a biscuit contained so much icing and a variety of sticky sweets. At least once the icing had dried, the biscuits had stayed intact although the shapes by now had become unrecognisable.

She knew however that her trusted friend Iris could cope amazingly with young children. She had two young grandchildren of her own that she helped look after on occasions. Molly was in no doubt that Iris would relish the idea.

"It would be lovely to be your judges" she lied. "Anything we can do to help in the community" she said to the ever so grateful teacher.

Cheryl Goodfellow explained that the pageant would take place on the last day of term when they delivered the cupcakes.

An excited Iris quickly turned her mind and hand to the making of small edible chocolate rabbits and sugar moulded chicks with eggs. As the order was so large Iris enlisted Molly's help with the decorations. Molly, not having the same dexterity as her friend, took longer to work the moulding sugar into the characters that Iris had created. She did however enjoy the challenge, and it was not long before she could equal Iris's artistic display of bunnies and chicks. Iris was delighted with her friend's perseverance and the outcome of the final product.

"You are amazing" said Iris, praising Molly's work. "Just wish I could learn to bake as well as you."

"You can bake equally as well I can" Molly told her friend plainly. "And on that note, I want to discuss with you about another idea I have had but you must be honest and say if you think it will be too much for us to do."

Iris was intrigued as she listened to her friend while she explained her new idea.

"I was wondering if we could introduce a couple of tray bakes to our cupcake selection" said Molly, who could already tell by her face that Iris was interested.

"I thought we could both choose one recipe each to start with, what do you think, Iris?"

Iris did not need to think twice and thought it was a great idea. She already had favourite recipe ideas flowing through her head.

"Can I work on a crunchy oat recipe that my mother use to make" said Iris hoping Molly would agree to her suggestion.

"Absolutely you can. And I thought I might work on a chocolate brownie recipe, what do you think?"

It was agreed that after Easter when they were less busy, they should each make their chosen tray bake and test out on each other and rope in their partners for tasting.

Until then they had a great deal of work to do to complete the current orders.

When the cakes were finished, Simon once again photographed the delicious display of cupcakes they had produced.

It would be the Thursday before Good Friday and as well as delivery day the women had time to prepare themselves for judging the school's junior classes Easter bonnet parade.

"Do you fancy taking a few hours out after we have made the deliveries and completed the judging" suggested Molly.

"I thought because we have been so busy, we could take a trip to the seaside for a picnic lunch." Iris's face lit up.

"Yes, that would be a lovely idea, but I insist on making the picnic for us both" said Iris who was excited about the prospect of a trip to the seaside.

Chapter 2

B oth their respective partners were going to be working on that day before the Easter bank holidays. They had both been looking forward to another round or two of golf over the forthcoming long weekend so were pleased the girls had decided to take time out for themselves. This they had colluded between each other might offer the chance of them spending more time on the golf course without feeling guilty.

Rosie was loaded up with the boxes of cakes. Some of the boxes had been tied with colourful ribbons as was usually the case. Iris checked each labelled box carefully with the corresponding orders and addresses. They had become quite apt at this procedure ensuring the boxes were always loaded in the correct order for taking them out when they had reached their destinations. Cakes for the school had been placed at the rear as these would be the last ones to take out. As well as the cakes there was just enough room for Iris's picnic basket, large flask, and a picnic rug.

Molly and Iris often shared the driving. They knew that it was important just in case one or other of them had been unwell or indisposed. This day it would be Iris's turn to drive. Waving and tooting at people just as Molly would do, she felt immensely proud.

Once again, their deliveries were completed without a hitch. Their last destination was the school. Iris being Iris had made them both an Easter bonnet to wear. The pink straw hats had been decorated with bright coloured tissue paper flowers that could be secured under their chins with lengths of multi coloured ribbons.

"Is there no end to your talents?" said Molly admiring yet another one of Iris's crafts.

Having checked in with the school security, they delivered the cakes to the school canteen before being escorted by the secretary to the main hall. The sound of excited children could be heard from the corridor. Through the window they could see the staff helping the children to put on their own bonnets. Some looked as if they would be difficult to secure due to their shape and size. On closer inspection it was clear that a few of these hats had been crudely made by children who had not given any thought as to how they would be able to hold them on their heads. Other bonnets were so ornate that it was suspiciously thought by the teachers that the parents had made them. Some of whom might have thought themselves professional milliners. Molly wondered if prizes of chocolate Easter eggs were adequate for winners of these hat designers of the year. She smiled to herself as she made her way to the door.

With the doors open the noise was deafening but on seeing them arrive in Ms Goodfellow clapped her hands in a rhythm and the children responded, clapping their hands back with a shorter response and then they went quiet.

"I have got to learn that one!" Molly, who was so inspired by the sudden cessation of noise, whispered to Iris.

The teacher was in charge now.

"Come on children let's welcome the ladies from Molly's cupcakes who have kindly agreed to be our judges today."

A spontaneous enthusiastic applause greeted them both. In seconds it was brought abruptly to an end by a second rhythmic clapping routine, once again bringing the children back under control.

All the children were lined up in single file and equally spaced facing clockwise around the room. The judges were instructed to stand in the centre of the room. Iris was glad she had made them both a hat. Both teachers and their assistants were also wearing an assortment of Easter head gear. One assistant wore long pink fluffy ears. She had painted a black nose and whiskers completing her rabbit appearance. When all the children were ready the music began to blare out from the speakers, and they started to walk around the room to the song (The Easter Parade) sung by no other than Judy Garland and Fred Astaire. Within seconds hats were falling from heads and were quickly retrieved by teachers who hastily tried to help put them back on. This caused a sort of concertina pile up as child after child walked into each other knocking off more hats as they did so. Three children held them on not wanting to let them fall off. One little boy who refused to wear his hat had been made to carry it instead.

Molly and Iris had been in total agreement that they would choose the winners from what they thought to be child made hats rather than the elaborate ones that they believed a young child could not have made. Amongst the elaborate ones was a large boxed, chocolate egg. On top of this was situated a white rabbit with long ears. The whole thing looked as if it might topple off the child's head at any moment. To the relief of the children the music stopped, and they were all told to sit down on the floor. Iris and Molly were given another opportunity to walk around the circle of children and admire the funny and most obscure Easter hats that they had ever seen.

"This is an exceedingly difficult competition to choose winners" Molly said to the children diplomatically. "You have all done so well and your hats are amazing" she fibbed.

Ms Goodfellow came forward with certificates and small Easter eggs for Molly and Iris to hand out to the winners. There were three in all.

Iris chose who she thought would be one of the winners. She went over to the young child and spoke to her. The little girl was shy and nervously responded to Iris's questions. Her hat had a similarity to the ones she herself had made. The flowers on top were not perfectly made unlike their own but they did look as if the child had been involved in its creation. Iris returned to the centre of the floor having informed the teacher of her choice.

The teacher called out Hannah's name and she shyly made her way into the centre of the room where she immediately threw up onto the floor narrowly missing both Molly and Iris's clothes. It was fortunate that Iris had pulled Molly backwards and only just in time. Just a light splattering of vomit had reached their shoes. The child began to cry, and an assistant hastily removed Hannah out of the room to be cleaned up. A commotion erupted. A group of children started laughing and jeering but were immediately brought back to attention with another round of rhythmic clapping. The proceedings momentarily delayed while the smelly vomit on the floor was also cleaned up, including a quick wipe of their shoes. Molly noticed a few of the children pinching their noses attempting to mask the smell of vomit in the room. She herself, not having been in this situation before wanted to do the same. It took all her concentration to stop herself from urging in front of the children.

Unlike the children who had been told to remain seated on the floor, Molly and Iris felt able to take themselves to the outer circle where they attempted to converse with a few of the children. Pointing at and praising a particular piece of art that had caught their attention. Iris found talking to the children easier than Molly. She made light of the situation telling the children how brave she thought Hannah was. The children were beginning to show a degree of agitation, and another round of teacher-pupil clapping bought them back to order.

With the mess cleaned up, Molly and Iris returned to the middle of the circle where Molly quickly chose a little boy whose hat had been made from an egg box as the second winner. The hat was decorated like a birds' nest with straw on top. Adorning this were four painted eggs which on inspection she believed to be real blown hen eggs. They had appeared to have been varnished to help protect them from breaking. Once again, the name of the child was called out and he came forward joining his classmate who had been brought back into the room after the vomiting incident.

Their third choice was the little boy who had carried his creation rather than wearing it. The hat had been made using an old cereal box and had been decorated with coloured streamers and a banner that had spelt out Happy Easter. This was the young boy who thought he had no chance of winning and really did not care. One of the teachers had walked encouragingly beside him. Molly and Iris overheard him telling the teacher that "It's a stupid Easter hat competition." He knew his teacher was cross with him for not wearing his hat but there was no way he told her that he would put it on his head. On hearing his name called out the little lad boldly stepped forward. He was grinning from ear to ear and turned to give a cheeky look towards his teacher as he passed her by to collect his certificate and prize. Everyone applauded the winners. Ms Goodfellow thanked all the children for their extremely hard work in making such beautiful hats and thanked the judges for their time. Once again, the children followed the teachers in another round of applause. With a promise of a cupcake later that afternoon the children were uniformly marched out of the room and back to more formal lessons.

After a quick cup of instant coffee in the staff room Molly and Iris returned to their vehicle. From the glove box Molly took out a packet of wet wipes.

"Here you are Iris have some of these" she said, taking out a handful before passing the packet to Iris. After cleaning their hands, they both spent time wiping over their shoes again.

"Might help mask the smell!" said Molly.

"Poor child she couldn't help it," said Iris. "Just nervous, I guess!"

And Molly agreed.

Chapter 3

L eaving the school premises, they set off for the hour journey it took to get to the coast. The events of the morning being the main topic of conversation on the way.

Most tourists did not know Pearl Bay so on most days it could be a peaceful secluded haven. This day was no exception with only one other car parked on the beach. The two occupants were enjoying canoeing on the still calm water. Choosing the same spot as they had always chosen, Iris set out the blanket between two exceptionally large rocks giving them protection from the cross-shore breeze and privacy. Kicking off their shoes they quickly removed their socks before rolling up their trouser legs. Laughing, they raced each other past the car to the water's edge. Both wanting to be the first to paddle in the salt water in that new year.

"Wow! It's freezing" Iris shouts as the first gentle wave splashes over her feet.

"No skinny dipping yet" said Molly, recalling their antics of the previous summer when they had dared each other to strip off for a swim. However, that had been during the heat wave of July where there seemed no other way of cooling themselves down.

Molly let the water flow over her feet, covering her ankles, and gingerly walked further into the sea until the chilly water reached her calves. Another wave, this time a little stronger, caught Molly off guard and she reached for Iris's hand for stability. Together they paddled for a few more minutes.

"That's enough for me" Molly said, turning and running back up the beach to the blanket that they had laid out on the damp sand. Iris quickly followed. When the sun came out from behind a cloud, they began to feel its warmth. Protected by the rocks they shared the small towel that Iris had brought with her to dry their feet. Still in bare feet, Iris walked the short distance to retrieve the picnic basket and flask from the van.

"Can't believe it's only April" said Iris on her return ladened down with basket in one hand and flask in the other.

"No neither can I" replies Molly eagerly waiting to be served a hot cup of coffee. Iris had noticed that Molly had not emptied her last cup of coffee back at the school.

"Coffee?" asks Iris smiling teasingly at Molly.

She removed the screw top and started to pour the steamy liquid from the flask. Molly sniffed into the air as the pleasing aroma reached her nostrils.

Iris certainly knew how to pack a picnic, but she did not know how to pack a picnic for two! With hot coffee in one hand, they both tucked into thick bread sandwiches filled with slices of ham and salad, sausage rolls, large slices of quiche, crisps, and homemade pickled eggs. For afters there were homemade fruit pies and custard tarts. Two large rosy apples came out and went back into the basket. Molly accepted a second cup of coffee whilst Iris opted for a carton of fruit juice.

"I'm stuffed" said Molly, burping and apologising. "Thanks Iris that was lovely."

"You are very welcome; you are always cooking meals for us so it's nice to do something for you in return."

Iris packed up the remaining food before they both stretched out on the blanket to soak up the warm afternoon sun on their faces. It was not long before both women started to feel sleepy. Molly laid with her eyes closed listening to the mesmerising sounds of the sea. She thought she could distinguish the sound of the two people dragging their canoe up the beach and the soft tones of their voices. To her side she could hear the soft snoring breaths of her friend giving her cause to smile and then she too feeling relaxed fell asleep.

It was the sudden change in temperature that aroused the pair back to full wakefulness. The clear blue skies had been replaced by white cumulus clouds which were bubbling up and moving quite quickly across the sky. In the distance were darker clouds beginning to mass and move in their direction.

The ground underneath them felt cold through the blanket they were lying on.

"Wake up Molly" instructed Iris while nudging Molly in her side. "It's getting late, and the tide is coming in."

Molly shivered and rubbed her eyes before looking at her watch and realised the lateness of the day. Scrabbling to be upright just as the sea was about to wash over her sandy cold feet. Retrieving the now damp blanket and shoes they retreated a little further up the beach.

"Oh my God Iris! I cannot believe I fell asleep, I only meant to rest my eyes."

Molly and Iris hastily brushed as much of the sand off their feet as they could, before replacing their shoes. Now, unbeknown to them, the tide was not only coming in, but they had failed to notice a sandbar behind the rocks. The incoming tide was lapping at Rosie's tyres.

"Hells bells!" Iris shouts realising the predicament they were in.

Grabbing their remaining belongings, they hurried to Rosie's rescue, opening the back door, and throwing everything in. Jumping into the van with Molly taking the driving seat. Pushing the key into the ignition, Molly attempted to start the engine. Turning the key once and then again without success.

"Come on Rosie don't let us down now." Molly spoke nervously but encouragingly to the little van as she tried repeatedly to turn the key but to no avail.

Iris opened her door and got out. The water was now deep enough to cover her feet.

"Better get out, I think Rosie is stuck in the wet sand."

Grabbing their handbags, they sped quickly up the beach to dry ground leaving Rosie stranded. The situation was serious, but Molly could not help herself, placing her hand to her mouth to stifle a chuckle. There had been only a handful of times when Iris could not understand the behaviour of her friend, and this was one of them.

"Molly, how can you think it's funny" she said. "What about poor Rosie? And what are we going to do?"

"I'm sorry Iris, I know it's serious really, but you must agree it is a bit funny" she replies, smiling reassuringly at her.

It did not take long for Iris to accept the absurdness of the situation that they had found themselves in. She too gave way to a little titter. There was nothing they could do to save Rosie as the waves continued to lap at her wheels. With every retreating wave it was obvious that her wheels were sinking deeper into the wet sand. As if this was not enough of a problem it started to rain. A light drizzle at first which quickly turned to a much more, steadier, and heavier downpour. Once again, they would have to call on their partners to help them out.

An hour later from making the call, Simon arrived in his car. Shortly followed by Rob driving his tow truck. They were met by two very miserable women who were by now soaked and very cold. They stood draped together with what had become a sodden picnic blanket, and they looked to be in a sorry state.

This was no time for chastising their wives and the two men donned their waterproofs and boots and went into the water. Securing Rosie to the tow truck before gently pulling her out of the wet sand. If it had been any later the tide would have been well in, and Rosie would have had to wait until the tide had turned.

The women climbed into the back seat of Simon's car glad to be out of the rain. They were cold, wet, and shivering.

"Well girls!" said Simon, turning to face the bedraggled pair in his back seat and trying not to laugh at them. "That was quite a jolly day, wasn't it? I expect you would like a hot drink!"

From the front seat he produced a flask and two mugs. Molly swore it was the best coffee she had ever tasted.

A Merry Dance

Chapter 1

Following the trip to the seaside, Rosie was out of service for two weeks. It was to be of no surprise to Molly to learn there had been water in the van's electrics and the distributer cap had needed to be completely dried out. As well as an all over pressure wash to remove the salt. Under the circumstances Rosie had fared very well.

"It's a good job you knew not to keep trying to turn her over, because if you had you may have sucked sea water into the poor van's engine and there would have been a very different outcome." said Rob.

Molly pretended that she already knew about this but truthfully had no idea of how disastrous it could have been.

"Thanks Rob, I don't know what I would do without you" said Molly, slightly embarrassed by the whole scenario.

Rob was not only an excellent mechanic and car enthusiast he was also her and Simon's very dear friend and most definitely, Rosie's too.

Simon came to the rescue offering his car to 'Molly Monday's cupcakes' for delivery days until Rosie was back on the road.

Molly had expected Simon to be angry but to her surprise there had been no reprimand this time, however, he did seem to spend more time on the golf course over the holiday period and the weekends following this. Molly did not mind, it meant that this would give her more time to herself, and she could concentrate her thoughts on the new tray bakes that both she and Iris were planning to make.

Before this and with time to herself Molly decided spring cleaning was overdue. She decided to make a start in the rooms on the ground floor.

Taking with her a duster from underneath the kitchen sink Molly went into the study. The bookshelves had gathered a layer of thick dust. Over the years Molly and Simon had collected a vast amount of reference books which included music, cookery, and travel. As well as these there were shelves full of fiction. Both being enthusiastic readers. They had always tried to keep the books in some sort of catalogue order, but due to them both being so busy, this had recently been overlooked and the shelves had become higgledy-piggledy. This, Molly thought to herself, was going to be a good day for dusting and sorting their books.

Scanning the shelves Molly's eye was drawn to a tatty, dog-eared brown book that was near to the top of one of the shelves. Feeling inquisitive she dragged Simon's desk chair towards her so she could stand on it to reach the book. Immediately she saw it she realised it was a book from her earlier years. Wiping away the layer of dust to reveal the complete title she read the title "Sex in the Sixties" and giggled to herself as she remembered where the book had come from and what it had been about.

Molly had met Simon while at university, but he had not been her first boyfriend. Johnathan had been her first. Molly quickly came to realise that he had a one-track mind and had only been interested in her for sex. It had been just a matter of weeks into their relationship when he had tried it on with her and she had not felt ready to move on to the next stage as a courting couple. Where most boys would buy chocolates or flowers, he had chosen to buy Molly a book for her birthday. Not just any book it seems but one that would make her feel disappointed and embarrassed. How could she tell her parents or even her friends about the gift she had received from her boyfriend?

"It's a must-read Molly, very informative" Johnathan had said.

"Sex is nothing to be afraid of it's just a bit of fun!"

Molly, her virginity intact back in those early university days, was persuaded by Johnathan to read the book. She did not consider herself to be prudish by any means. The book had not revealed anything new to her other than the various positions one could have sex in. This she thought to herself, one would have to be a contortionist. Molly shared the book with her close girlfriends. They had spent some amusing girly evenings together browsing the diagrams and discussing the terminology of the content.

Her relationship with Johnathan was to be short lived. Molly had realised that they had extraordinarily little in common. Neither of them in anyway heartbroken when the split eventually came.

It was about a month later when Molly had been introduced to Simon. He had been playing the piano in a fundraising concert held in the university. Along with her housemates she had bought a ticket. Molly had seen him around the campus, and he was quite popular within his peer group. She had taken a fancy to him believing she had no chance of ever having a relationship with him. At that time unbeknown to her he had felt the same towards her. From the moment they had come together their friendship developed quickly into a serious and committed love affair. They had so much in common. Enjoying the same taste in foods and music as well as travel and ambition.

It had been some years into their marriage when Molly had come across the book again. It had been in a box of assorted things that she had been going through for a jumble sale. Dusting it off before showing it to Simon.

One evening after sharing a bottle of wine, having had a couple of beers as well, and when they were both feeling a little tipsy, they decided to try out the positions that were illustrated in the little brown book. Manoeuvring into position before falling about and laughing.

"Who needs a book to tell us how to do it!" Simon had said "Especially, when I have the perfect woman in my arms."

In those early years Molly often teased Simon about how romantic he was and how he could give Byron a run for his money. He was also a generous lover. Always considerate of her needs as well as his own. Once he had written her a love poem. Putting it to music he sang it to her whilst playing along on his piano. They both agreed it was the worst love song ever written and would go to the top of the charts should someone famous record it.

Returning to the task in hand and smiling to herself Molly put the book to one side thinking she would show it to Simon later. "Who knows perhaps this is just what I need to rekindle my sex life" she mused.

Among her countless recipe books which Molly had collected over the years, some of which had belonged to her mother and were one of her most treasured possessions, Molly had an ample collection of folders that she had accumulated from her time at university.

Many of these contained papers and articles covering subjects she had studied. The collective terminology being that of domestic science. This she had studied as part of her degree. Among the folders she found one which she had decorated its cover in pictures of well-known rock bands that she had followed and had enjoyed listening to in her teens. The contents of this folder included notes on recipe adaptations, and papers of scribbled practice ones. One piece of tatty looking paper fell out of the folder onto the floor. Retrieving it she unfolded its creases revealing what she had named (Molly's fairy brownies) making her smile.

"Oh! My goodness" Molly thought to herself as she began to read the list of ingredients that she had written on the piece of paper. "Not sure I can use this one again" she continued, speaking aloud to herself. She had forgotten about the special butter that she had concocted and used to make the brownies for a party that had been held on campus. They had been so popular within her group of friends that Molly had been asked to make them again for other parties.

Putting the recipe to one side Molly continued to clean and sort the bookshelves into some order. This had been her challenge for the day, and she was eager to complete the work so she could plan her baking.

***

With orders up to date as well as the paperwork, Molly phoned Iris to discuss a suitable day for them to bake and in agreement set aside the following afternoon for their experimental baking.

Molly spent the rest of the day in preparation. She collected the eggs and went through the list of ingredients that both she and Iris would need ensuring a good supply of everything, just in case mixtures needed to be tweaked. Chocolate brownies had always been a favourite one of Molly's to make so she expected it to be an easy assignment for herself.

The following afternoon the women set to work and their individual challenge. Measuring and mixing their ingredients until the first batch was ready for baking.

"Let's have a coffee, or would you prefer tea Iris?" asked Molly.

"I think I would rather have tea if that's ok" Iris replied.

Molly busied herself making the beverages for them both.

"I have something to show you" said Molly, taking out the book from the drawer that she had found earlier and offering it to Iris.

"Oh my! Molly, where did you get it from" asks Iris, flicking through the pages of pencil like drawings before turning the book at different angles to see the images differently.

Molly told Iris the story of how she had found it on the bookshelf when she had been cleaning and then went on to tell the story of how it had come into her possession.

"I don't think I could do this one" Iris laughed pointing out one of the diagrams and reading the 'so called' benefits at the same time. "I never did enjoy athletics at school" she said.

"I was thinking I might try this one" Molly said, turning the pages to find the one she was looking for to show Iris.

The two of them were laughing so loudly that it brought attention to Simon who had just returned home and had to peek in at them to see what the laughter was all about.

"It's ok Si" said Molly, "I will show you later tonight." And this causing Iris to laugh even more loudly.

Molly placed the book back in the drawer. There was just enough time for a second beverage for them both before the timer buzzed indicating the cakes were cooked.

To their delight both tray bakes had turned out well. The tasting would have to wait until the cakes had cooled down.

Having cleaned up the kitchen it was time for the tasting. Both agreed that the two recipes had turned out well. However, Molly decided that she wanted to try adding a vanilla cream marble effect to the centre of the brownies and add some cherries. Iris wanted to try adding a marzipan layer in between the sweet oat bake.

They had just enough time to bake another batch each before stopping for the day. So keen to get the perfect mixture that they chose to work in silence. Weighing, mixing, and beating their ingredients all the while jotting down notes as they went. The final batch turned out even better than expected and they were both delighted.

"Glad that's done. Think we both deserve a cuppa. Just need to give them a name though," said Molly.

"I know what I will call mine," said Iris. "Marzi Oat Slice. That is if its ok with you Mol."

"Absolutely you can. They are your creation, so you can name it whatever you like. And I will call the brownies, Cherry Marbled Brownies. There! That's sorted."

Chapter 2

The third Saturday of the month of May was the annual May Day celebrations for the village. As was usual the farmers market and local traders would set up stalls in the street and all around the square. A Morris group local to the area would be invited to dance in the square as were the children chosen from the primary school to show off their skills at maypole dancing.

Molly had once again applied to hold her own stall for the event, and again the local council had granted this.

As was customary Molly and Iris with their partners met with other friends in the pub on the Friday evening before. On this occasion the Morris men would play music and sing songs in the bar for all to enjoy with the occasional solo jig danced by one of them.

Placing the tray of drinks on the table Jenny the bartender enquired as to whether Molly was going to dance a jig tonight like she had on the previous year.

"Not tonight, Jenny, I must keep a clear head tonight. Iris and I are holding a cake stall tomorrow and will need to set up early" said Molly smiling, as she recalled how she and Iris the previous year had danced with two of the Morris men trying to copy a jig whilst waving hankies at the same time.

"That's exciting Mol" says Jenny. "I shall look forward to buying some cakes from your stall tomorrow."

"We have also made some tray bakes as well as our usual selection this year haven't, we Iris," said Molly.

"Yes, so hoping for bigger sales," Iris grins.

From across the room Iris returned a little wave to PP who took this as an invitation for her and Michael to join them at their table.

"Look out Mol, PP is on her way" Iris whispered to her friend.

Simon retrieved two more chairs and welcomed them into the group.

"We have only been to this pub for a meal before" Michael tells them. "And jolly good food if I might say so" he continued.

"Yes" agreed Pru. "It was Jenny who suggested we might enjoy this evening. Are you sure you don't mind if we join you? We don't know many people here yet."

"Of course, you're welcome to join us" replies Molly.

"Let me get you some drinks. What's your poison?" asks Rob.

A little cough from Iris and a grin from Molly reminded Rob of the last time they had all been together. Taking their orders he went to the bar.

It was to be another great fun evening at their local. Everyone having had a few drinks began to relax. This time it was PP who was easily cajoled into joining in with the Morris dancing having declared that she had danced with a female Morris set years ago when she had lived in Kent. Much to everyone's amazement she turned out to be an incredibly good dancer. Customers in the bar stood to applaud her which she accepted graciously.

"There's a lot we don't know about PP" said Molly to Iris as she clapped her enthusiastically.

When it was time for last orders David came over to their table to tell them that he was having a lock in and that they were welcome to stay on. There would be a half a dozen other friends that had also been invited to stay behind. Molly knew it was a bad idea and that she and Simon had to be up early to set up the tent covering for the stall the following morning. But when she had had a few drinks, it was easy to give in believing she would have the energy to cope the following day.

Customers drifted off leaving a dozen or so remaining in the bar. The Morris men also bid farewell after singing a traditional departing song.

The six friends now moved closer to the bar where they continued conversing with other friends. David locked the door before offering free drinks to the remaining people left.

"I must make this the last one Iris," said Molly. "We have a busy day tomorrow."

Molly knew that everything was ready at home, it was just the matter of setting up and displaying their wares on the table. It was important to them that everything should appear professional. This they knew could be good for business.

One last drink always seemed to turn into one more and then another until everyone was more than a little inebriated.

David and Sacha at last called the evening to an end and walked the last few people to the door. Bidding farewell to everyone Sacha reminded them to keep the noise down.

"We don't want any complaints" she said holding a finger to her lips. "Especially if we want to be able to do this again."

The church clock chimed one o'clock as they stepped outside. As is usually the case being quiet is not always easy especially when one in the group manages to trip over the threshold as the door is closed behind them. It was fortunate that Michael's quick reaction managed to prevent Al from falling flat on his face.

"Hey! Look over there" said PP, excitedly pointing to the pole on the green. To which everyone put a finger to their lips to shush her. "I know how to maypole dance; come on everyone I will teach you."

There was so much more to PP than anyone realised.

Astonished by her drunken repose and her enthusiasm to share her skill it was difficult not to follow her. The six who had shared a table along with Al and Stuart as well as Jenny and her friend Jack followed PP. Arm in arm and giggling, they crossed the road in the darkness onto the village green.

"Come on everyone grab one of these and let's be boy girl around the pole" instructed the bossy dance tutor as she untied the ribbons and handed everyone an end to hold on to. Handing one to Al she saw that he was with Stu and looked around the circle.

"Oh well you will just have to pretend to be a girl" she says to Stuart handing him a red ribbon. Amused by this everyone else started laughing. They all knew that Stu and Al were in a relationship accept that is, PP.

"Come on everyone be serious and follow my instructions. It's quite simple and when I call out your colour you dance clockwise around or anti clockwise when I say so."

Everyone knew the ribbons would have been made up of vibrant colours but in the dark, and when the moon disappeared behind the clouds it was difficult to distinguish between them.

As instructed, everyone began to move around the pole. Each one holding a ribbon and trying hard to stop themselves from laughing aloud. It did not take long for all the dancers to get themselves tangled up. No amount of tuition was going to help the situation. PP was getting cross with her students which made the situation even more farcical. On one side of the circle Jenny fell over and Jack fell on top of her. While on the other side Rob collided with Iris. Everyone was in fits of laughter except PP who continued to try and untangle the knots that they had made.

It was only when across the street that lights started to go on in upstairs windows that everyone began to panic and disperse for fear of being caught. Michael had to pull Pru away, but she struggled with him determined to continue. The six of them eventually left the green to walk the mile or so back to their homes. The remaining taking themselves in the opposite direction.

None could walk a straight line. Simon took charge of PP supporting her by taking her arm through his own. Every few steps she started to skip and was trying to show off how well she could dance. It became quite difficult for Simon to keep her upright and he moved closer to Rob who took her other arm. Molly and Iris each took one of Michael's arms so as not to leave him walking on his own.

"Oh look" said PP as she tried to encourage her two gallant knights as she referred to them. "We look like we are walking the yellow brick road, come on" she said, "join in boys, follow me" as she tried to get them to polka along the road singing "we're off to see the wizard."

It was past two in the morning by the time they reached their homes. Michael took his wife's hand and led her up the garden path. By now she had become a little quieter.

"Someone's going to have a hangover tomorrow!" said Rob as the four watched as PP was escorted by her husband safely into their house.

"See you about seven!" whispered Molly kissing Iris goodnight.

"Not much sleep tonight but I'm sure we will manage."

The men agreed to meet at six thirty to load Simon's car with the canopy and furniture that they needed to make up the stall. The women planned to load Rosie and follow on a little later giving the men time to set up.

Chapter 3

The following morning came round far too quick for Molly. She had not heard Simon get up, but she was grateful for the aroma of the mug of coffee he had left on her bedside table along with two paracetamol tablets. Molly had not remembered asking for them, but she was grateful for these too.

Looking at the clock she realised that it was late, and that Iris would be knocking at the door soon. Quickly she drank the lukewarm coffee swallowing the pills along with it. In minutes she had showered and dressed but there was no time for breakfast. From a tin she took a handful of assorted bars of chocolate and placed them in her handbag. Something, she thought to herself, to munch on later.

Iris knocked on the door but as was usually the case let herself in. Molly gawped at her as she noticed her very black eye.

"Don't say a word" she said. "Rob's got a shiner too, we bashed into each other when we were doing that stupid dancing last night. Had no idea it was such a hard knock. The alcohol must have numbed the pain."

All four friends had degrees of hangovers and knew they just had to get through the day the best they could.

Quietly but efficiently, they set up their stall displaying cupcakes and slices of the new tray bakes to sell. On the green they could see the dreaded maypole. The junior school head teacher Mrs Marden, with help from Cheryl Goodfellow and others, were trying to untangle the ribbons. There was a great deal of angry raised voices heard where people had gathered to see what had been going on. George Johnson along with his wife Wendy, who had a dairy stall next to Molly Munday's cupcakes, came over and explained that a group of youths had been spotted playing with it late last night. Mrs Marden was furious and had contacted the head of the senior school blaming some of the students that she thought had more than likely been responsible.

Having sorted out the tangled mess the young children from the primary school, dressed in their PE kit and divided into two groups, were ready to show off their maypole dancing skills. Half wore red sashes while the other half wore yellow. The small children were placed in position around the circle and given a ribbon each to hold. Proud relatives and friends drew closer to watch. The music started and Ms Goodfellow called out instructions and the dancing commenced. Molly and Iris joined the crowd. No one was going to buy anything from the stalls while the dancing was taking place.

"Aren't they amazing Iris," said Molly. "So clever!"

"Perhaps if we had sashes, we might have done better" Iris whispered in Molly's ear. They both chuckled and clapped the children's performance.

Back at their stall Mrs Marden approached them. She chose to buy six cupcakes and two slices from each of the tray bakes praising them both for their quality goods.

"Well-done to you as well for the lovely maypole dancing. The children did you proud as usual," said Molly.

"Thank you but it is Ms Goodfellow who must take all the credit. She is responsible for the dance tuition. She has worked so hard."

"She certainly has" agreed both.

"And I'm not going to rest until I have found the culprits who nearly ruined everything" she told them angrily. "They spoilt it for the little ones who I might add have been practising for weeks."

And with tongue in cheek, they both agreed as she walked away from the stall carrying her box of cakes.

Wendy from her dairy stall approached them.

"I must buy some of your cakes Molly before you sell them all. They look so delicious I don't know which to choose."

Turning her attention towards Iris and having already seen Rob, Wendy asked how they had both managed to get a black eye.

"Silly really" said Iris with a straight face. "We had a little tiff, he hit me, so I hit him back."

Wendy's face was a picture until Iris and Molly started to laugh.

More customers started to arrive and were keen to buy a selection of cakes, so this put an end to the conversation about the black eyes.

The cupcakes as always were a great hit, and the new slices of tray bakes were also a success. The photographs that Simon had taken had been enlarged into colourful posters depicting a variety of cakes that Molly Munday's business could supply. As well as selling everything they had to offer they picked up several more orders as well.

In the distance on the green Molly could see PP and her husband seated on a bench. Taking two slices of cake and stopping to buy two cups of tea she walked over to the couple.

"Here you go you two, thought you might like to try our new cakes."

Bending down to PP who appeared to be a bit embarrassed she whispered in her ear "Great night last night. Thanks for making it such fun" and dropped a little kiss on her very pale cheek. PP smiled.

The Vicar's Tea Party

Chapter 1

Molly woke early after an exceptional sleep. The hormonal replacement therapy that she had been taking for the last few days seemed to have kicked in or just maybe it was the unexpected exceptional love making of the night before. Molly regretted not making the appointment with Dr Foster sooner. She could not believe how much better she felt about herself. Even the sheets were dry.

"Of course, I would still like you to cut down on your caffeine and alcohol intake. Have you tried decaffeinated coffee? There are some excellent brands out there now" suggested Dr Foster. "And I will also need to keep an eye on your blood pressure, it's just a bit higher than normal."

"That was most probably due to the fact that I was sitting in his surgery and feeling extremely uncomfortable at being there" Molly was thinking to herself having turned her nose up to the suggestion of decaff coffee.

From her bed Molly could hear Simon in the kitchen below stairs and she could already smell the aroma of the freshly made coffee that he was preparing for breakfast. She stretched her legs and rolled over to turn off the alarm before it sounded and waited eagerly for her drink.

Simon entered the bedroom grinning from ear to ear and handed her the steaming mug of coffee.

"You look happy this morning" she remarked.

"Yes, I just had a 'flash back' from last night" he said cheekily as he leant over her and planted a kiss on her forehead.

Molly took her first sip of the hot liquid.

"Yuk!" she exclaimed "What the hell is this? I can't drink this, it's not our usual" she said handing the mug back to Simon.

"The doctor said you had to cut back on caffeine so I thought we could try this new one that I bought yesterday from the supermarket."

"I don't think so!" Molly heatedly replied. "At least not the first one of the day!"

Such was Molly's dissatisfaction; her mood changed and became one of agitation and she could feel a hot flush coming on and started to fan herself with her hand.

"Alright Mol, I was only trying to help, I will go and make you another."

Molly felt a bit guilty for her outburst and apologised to which Simon humbly accepted. When he had left the room, she quickly got out of bed, showered, and dressed.

On entering the kitchen, she was handed a fresh mug of her usual coffee, and it came with a smile and a kiss. After sipping it she began to feel better more like her new self.

"I will try and alternate between our usual and the decaf" she said smiling.

Things were quiet on the baking front, so Iris had taken a few days off and had gone to visit her son and daughter in law and their two children.

It was on these occasions that Molly had sometimes wished that her own daughter and partner had lived closer to her. Their daughter Laura had met her French partner during her time at university. Laura had been studying languages and just like her parents, she had loved to travel. It was inevitable that following their graduation, they would choose to live and work in France.

Molly and Simon tried to visit as often as they could, and they enjoyed these holidays immensely. Molly was also able to facetime Laura frequently and this made them feel closer. Molly would often receive small gifts from France including the odd baking specialities that she had been unable to purchase at home.

Molly had decided to spend the day catching up on her paperwork and restocking the cupboards. She always bought the basic ingredients for her business from the cash and carry. The more intricate ones had to be ordered in especially. Eggs however were always in plentiful supply thanks to her small brood of hens at the bottom of the garden.

That morning the postal worker knocked on the door; in his hand he held a small parcel.

"Difficult to read the label properly, it's got a bit damp" he said. "It has your name on it, but the address is a bit obscure, but it has come from France" he continued excitedly. "So, I think it must be from your Laura."

Kevin- known to everyone as Kev-was the postal worker who had been delivering mail on the same round for several years. Being from a local family he knew all the addresses in the area.

Thanking him she took the parcel inside eager to open it. On examination she did not think the handwriting was that of her daughter. It was addressed to an M. Monday which was a bit obscure. The address itself was she agreed difficult to decipher. Some of the wording appeared to have been smudged. It was quite possible that the heavy downpours of rain over the last couple of days had caused the ink to run. Tearing open the package revealed a brown envelope but no letter. She thought this odd as Laura would always include a brief note with any package she would send from France. Carefully Molly opened the envelope. Inside she found a small plastic pouch containing dried herbs of some kind. Her first reaction was one of unfamiliarity to the contents until she took a sniff and then the 'penny dropped' and she let the small package drop to the floor. No way she thought to herself, had this package come from her daughter, and there is definitely no way that the package has been intended for her.

"How bizarre" she thought to herself wondering where it had come from and who the recipient might have been. "Quite unbelievable" she thought to herself having only recently come by her old recipe for fairy brownies.

That evening she showed Simon the envelope and he agreed that he too would have also initially assumed the package had come from their daughter Laura.

Simon just like Molly knew instantly that the contents of the package was indeed from the cannabis plant. It had only been a few weeks ago when he himself had picked up a small packet containing a similar amount of the stuff off the corridor floor in college. When he had challenged his students as to whom it had belonged, naturally, there had been no response. He thought to himself at the time that he may have returned it if the owner had come forward. Hadn't he dabbled occasionally when he was of a similar age to those of his students? It is strange, he had thought to himself, that as a parent and especially as a teacher his views had changed on the matter and the recreational weed, he knew, could be dangerous, and should be discouraged.

After he deliberated as to whether he should keep it for himself, he dutifully handed the package in to the college principal who told him he would see that it was destroyed. To this day Simon was not sure just how the principal had intended to get rid of the weed! He was a little suspicious!

After supper that evening and with a glass of wine in their hand, they sat reminiscing about their student days and what they had got up to.

"Do you remember Mol when you made those special cakes" asks Simon with a twinkle in his eye.

Molly told him about how coincidentally she had come across the recipe again when she had been cleaning the study.

"It brought back lots of happy memories," said Molly as she cuddled closer to Simon.

"Do you think you could still remember how to make them?"

"I'm sure I can, at least I would love to have a go" she grinned. "Do you think I should try it?" asked Molly thinking that it was most unlikely that they could find the owner of the cannabis and return it to them.

They both agreed that Molly should have a go just for a bit of fun.

"After all it won't be harming anybody else" said Simon who was quite excited about the prospect of trying Molly's special cakes again.

"Not just cakes!" she replied with a grin. "Fairy Brownies!"

Chapter 2

The following day a happy Molly set to work making her special brownies.

"Alexa, play songs from the Bee Gees" she requested. The request having been accepted, the music commenced, and Molly started to join in with the familiar songs.

"Alexa, volume up." Once again Alexa obliged.

Molly had already decided to make her brownies by hand just as she had done when she had been at university. Swaying her hips in time to the music and singing at the top of her voice while beating the mixture together brought back memories of her carefree youth. The last thing she had wanted was for the phone to ring, interrupting her happy thoughts, but Molly knew she would have to answer its persistent ring.

"Alexa off" she shouted again at the machine as she stopped what she had been doing and walked quickly across to her desk to answer the call.

"Hello, is that Molly? I hope I am not disturbing you," came the voice on the other end of the phone. "It's Tom here, I wonder if you might be able to help me out?"

"Molly are you there? Can you hear me?"

Molly's heart was racing, and her mouth suddenly became dry.

"Yes, reverend, I am here" she spoke hoping her voice did not sound too shaky. "What is it I can do for you?"

The Reverend Thomas Cutler was the local vicar. Born and raised locally like Molly. They had attended the same schools and been friends. Molly's parents used to tease her referring to him as her boyfriend which would upset her.

Tom had been by far the most good-looking boy in the school, and he knew it. As if being born beautiful had not been enough he boasted a confidence that she and many of her friends in her class had envied. In primary school they had been best friends and inseparable but by the time they reached secondary school things began to change. Tom's popularity continued especially with the girls. He knew he could have the pick of any girl he chose. Molly though never felt that way about him and much as Tom tried, he could never persuade her to become his one and only as he called it.

They both moved on when she left for university, and Tom like his father had a calling and chose to study theology. After his studies were complete, Tomas Cutler was ordained into the church.

It was some years later and Molly's mother had written to her informing her that he was now the vicar of their parish.

Molly, unlike her mother, was not a regular church attender but, on the odd occasion, when visiting home, she would always accompany her mother to church. Meeting Tom again had been pleasant. He introduced her to his very pretty wife Louise who Molly took an instant like to and thought they were well suited. A perfectly handsome couple.

Before Tom had married, he had sought Molly's company on more than one occasion. He had offered to take her out for old times' sake, and she had refused. By this time, her engagement to Simon was well known.

It was rumoured that Tom was a bit of a flirt, just as he had been in his youth, but most said it was just his way of being friendly. His pastoral catchphrase of "bless you" became synonymous and well known amongst the community. So much so that a few of his flock could sometimes be seen taking the micky, blessing each other when they had passed in the street.

His wife Louise was a very shy sort of person. Not a great mixer other than when it had anything to do with the church. Her time was taken up between duties within the parish as the vicar's wife and the bringing up of their two children.

"Molly, I do wish you would call me Tom. We have been friends for so many years, how are you keeping? Have not seen you in church recently. I hope everything is ok."

"Couldn't be better thank you" she replied haughtily knowing full well she had not attended church since Christmas or seen him since his Christmas party. "Just been so busy!"

"Well, that's good news then Molly" he said, then clearing his throat to continue: "I know it's not what your business usually does but I have been let down and need someone to cater for a small afternoon tea party, just a few sandwiches, perhaps some small pastries and of course some of your famous cupcakes."

Molly never liked to turn work away but, in this instance, she had never felt more tempted to make an exception, but her Christian morals would not allow her to do so.

"Let me get my diary and note pad and see what I can do for you" said Molly obligingly knowing full well they had only a few small orders for the remainder of that month.

Molly put down the receiver and deliberately took her time to retrieve the paperwork she needed knowing the papers were already there in front of her.

"Right vicar! I'm ready"

"Ready for what I wonder!" came the reply. A slight pause before he continued. "To business, it was going to be an ecumenical tea party in our garden until my wife decided to include the ladies from the guild. So, catering for about twenty people."

Molly knew she should have discussed this with Iris before accepting the booking but believed her friend would be willing to help her. Iris was due home the following day, so Molly knew she would have plenty of time that evening to make plans. But then came the next bomb shell!

"It would be wonderful if you could also supervise the party yourself, serve the food, and make cups of tea and if it is not too much to ask, to clean up afterwards, just to save my wife from having to do it. Naturally, I will pay for the extras."

Standing with the phone to her ear and her mouth open, Molly could not respond quickly and felt the need to sit down.

"Oh dear!" came the voice on the other end following what he considered to be a long pause. "Am I asking too much of you Molly?"

"No Vicar, I'm sure we can manage something for you" she replied through gritted teeth.

"You are wonderful Mol; I don't know what I would have done if you had said no."

He had never called her Mol before, and she was taken aback by his casual reference to her name.

"Are you sure you can manage? You sound a bit hesitant."

"No Tom it's fine. I just need a little more detail" said Molly trying to sound professional.

"Tom sounds much better and less informal don't you think?"

"What date have you in mind?" she asked opening her pad with one hand to a clean piece of paper.

"Well. That is the other thing Mol" he replied before dropping yet another bomb shell. "It's this Saturday so I know it might be short notice for you."

It most definitely was, she thought to herself. Didn't he realise the preparation that she would need?

"That will be ok. I work with an amazing team" said Molly, thinking she was deliberately bragging to a man of the cloth. Then on the other hand she thought to herself, with Iris and both their partners they were indeed an amazing team.

Molly wrote down all the details as the vicar explained about how she could use crockery and anything else she needed from the church hall. Arrangements were concluded including the handing over of the hall keys to her in plenty of time before the event.

"That all sound fine Vicar. You can leave it with me" Molly spoke formally and reassuringly before ending her end of the conversation.

"I could kiss you, Molly Munday! Thank you." Molly felt herself blush as she hung up the phone.

A strong cup of coffee or two was needed before Molly could digest what she realised she had taken on and with only three days to do it in. It was a good thing that Iris was coming home the following morning she thought to herself. Molly did however decide to phone her friend that evening to warn her of the challenge she had set them. Iris as usual was very reassuring.

Chapter 3

Molly finished off making her fairy brownies as best she could. Her mind reeling with the multitude of things that she had to do. She was still pleased with the result. They tasted just as they did all those years ago if not better.

Feeling more confident in herself for reasons only she would know, it was time to put the scribbled information that she had taken down from the vicar and make a more detailed list. Then she could plan the vicar's tea party ensuring its success.

Later that afternoon Simon, who had returned home from his afternoon lectures, was eager to try the cakes. He knocked and entered Molly's office to enquire if they were ready. He was not disappointed. The cakes were cooling on a rack. The familiar tantalising aroma wafted up his nose.

"I'll put the kettle on, shall I?" he suggested having quickly kissed Molly as he always would on returning from work.

Simon always took tea during the afternoon, preferably with a large slice of cake while Molly, who would occasionally take tea, decided she wanted a coffee.

He soon returned with a tray containing a small pot of tea for himself, milk jug, cup, and saucer. There was also a mug of coffee for Molly. Seating themselves at the work bench they sampled the freshly made double chocolate brownies that she had baked with the secret ingredient. Molly knew she had to keep a clear head so ate a small piece explaining to Simon the phone call she had had from the vicar that morning. It had been many years since they had both eaten the small squares of cake and did not know how they would react to them. Both agreed that the baking had been a success, and the brownies tasted delicious. The afternoon tea break went on longer than Molly had intended. Simon had finished his tea, and the effects of the brownies began to show.

"Let me help you with the washing up Mol" he offered, gathering the crockery together hastily causing a clash of two plates resulting in the breakage of one.

"Oh dear! Sorry Mol" he said.

From the tone of his voice and by the grin on his face his apology did not come across as very sincere. Molly smiled. She set to and washed the cups and remaining plate. Simon, with a tea towel in his hand, put his arms around her waist and started showering her neck with little kisses. Molly, who did not want her amorous husband to go any further, pushed him gently away.

"I really must get on. There is so much I must organise before Iris gets home" she said, giving him a little kiss before steering him out of her office.

"Guess I better get on myself, lots to do, but I think I might just close my eyes for ten before that" he said with a grin.

Molly, thankful she had only eaten a morsel of brownie compared with what Simon had eaten, smiled to herself before preparing for the following day's baking.

Chapter 4

The following morning Molly had just finished gathering the eggs from the bottom of the garden when Iris arrived. She had already been prepped by her friend for the task that lay in front of them. They hugged. This was something they had always done when they had been apart.

"Iris, I have been thinking! What do you think about us asking PP if she would like to help us with this one?" Molly waited for the suggestion to sink in.

Iris thought for a moment before she replied: "I think it would be a clever idea. We have not got long to prepare, and another pair of hands would be especially useful."

Molly suggested that they could ask PP if just this once she would like to help by making the pastries and sandwiches due to the event being short notice for them. Iris was happy to go along with that.

"When you ask her, don't forget to tell her no seafood though" said Iris jovially. "Remember what happened at her party."

PP was delighted and excited to be asked by Molly to help them.

"I can come straight away" PP replied hastily. "That is if you need me to."

"Thank you Pru that would be wonderful."

Since the May Day celebrations, Pru had warmed to the pair. She found herself a little jealous of their close friendship, so this was an opportunity to get to know them better. And she also believed herself to be the expert when it came to pastry making.

Stopping only for a quick break and a sandwich lunch the three of them worked well into the evening. An incredibly happy PP working as part of the team.

As usual the results were amazing. Cupcakes were decorated and tray bakes cut into shapes. PP made three types of pastry and worked the dough into delicate small pastry cases. While they had been baking in the ovens, she set to and had made the fillings. Lastly, they all worked together preparing sandwich fillers ready for the sandwiches that would be made fresh the following morning.

Molly was initially concerned that PP might be an annoyance in her kitchen as she did like to chat. However, her fears were allayed as PP worked quietly. She was a perfectionist in her art of pastry making and did not want to give Molly any cause to regret having asked her to help them.

"You never know" she said to her husband that evening. "Molly might want me to join Molly's Cupcakes permanently. After all no one can make pastry like I can!"

"Do not go getting any ideas about that. You might be disappointed. Even though I know you make the best pastries" he said dropping a reassuring kiss on top of her head. Mike was pleased that Pru had become better acquainted with Molly and Iris. He liked them both and got on well with their husbands. Overall, he thought, they were becoming closer friends. Mike observed his wife as she sat to the table going through her cookery books. She was smiling and humming a tune as she turned the pages, stopping when she found a recipe that she had been looking for. When Pru was happy then he was happy too.

Chapter 5

The day of the vicar's tea party was upon them. Molly made plans for Iris and PP to complete the sandwiches before packing everything into appropriate boxes ready for transportation. Iris along with PP would drive Rosie with the food to the venue. Meanwhile she would drive Simon's car to the village hall and collect the things that she thought they might need to serve the food and make the beverages.

Molly found it heavy work carrying the boxes to the car. Stopping at times to wipe her sweaty brow and take a few deep breaths as hot flushes came and went. With the task completed she drove the short distance to the vicarage with all the car windows wound down

Iris and PP arrived just ahead of her and were already emptying the van of its trays of food.

In plenty of time the buffet was arranged on the tables which had been dressed by the vicar's wife. Louise had also made small flower arrangements for decoration. In the corner was a separate table containing a selection of wine and soft drinks. Various size drinking glasses had been artfully arranged on a small separate table next to this.

Two members of the guild had offered their services to serve the drinks. Molly had been grateful for this. Molly and her staff changed into fresh pink coats with white aprons which had embroidered logos for Molly Munday's Cupcakes.

The handsome reverend Cutler in his usual superior, self-confident manner, walked into the room. Both Iris and Pru were beaming from ear to ear.

"Molly, you have exceeded yourself, I don't know how I will be able to thank you enough" said the vicar, taking Molly by her elbows and kissing both her cheeks while she had been carrying a large tray of cakes to the table. Once again, she found herself blushing and was cross with herself.

"Bless you all" he said turning his attention towards Iris and Pru. "Don't you all look pretty in your pink uniforms." And then with arms outstretched he made his way across to where they were standing to kiss them too. Behind his back Molly raised her eyebrows and smiled at Iris who tried to withdraw from the advancing vicar. She was not quick enough. She endured a hug as well as the kissing of both pink cheeks. PP thought this show of affection had been quite normal under the circumstances and as part of the team was extremely grateful to be included.

The guests started to arrive promptly at three o'clock. Molly knew or recognised some of the people from the village. Living in a small village, it was easy to double up by being a member of the guild as well as a flower arranger or bell ringer or even a sidesman.

Although she recognised two of the local clergy like the Roman Catholic priest and the Methodist minister, she did not know them so well.

PP oversaw the teas and coffees while Molly and Iris mingled between the guests' carrying trays of savoury and sweet treats to tempt the party guests. The vicar made a brief welcoming speech. Molly saw the vicar whisper into his wife's ear. She blushed and appeared a little embarrassed. In a soft and slightly quivering voice she began to make her own little speech.

"I would also like to especially welcome the members of the church guild and thank them for all their hard work. The list of charitable events and jobs which they undertake within our parish are too numerous to mention." This was followed by a rapturous round of applause accompanied by Hear! Hears! from the gathering.

"Lastly, I would like to say a big thank you to Molly and her team. At such short notice they have managed to provide us with what looks like a scrumptious afternoon tea." This followed by a second round of clapping.

"Tuck in everyone and enjoy yourselves. And do not forget to introduce yourselves to each other" concluded the vicar.

The vicarage garden was a delight to behold. The summer bedding flowers were in full bloom and the diverse collection of rose bushes already bursting with colourful and scented blooms. The recently mowed lawns extended down to the less formal part of the garden. The vicar explained to them that it was his set aside wild garden. The longer variety of grasses and tall multicolours of the wildflowers swayed in the warm afternoon breeze. Molly thought it looked enchanting. Almost magical.

Molly looked around at the guests and noticed they all were relaxing and getting on well. The conversations between them seemed to be changing from one of formal to more friendlier tones. There seemed to be more laughter, and the talking was becoming a bit louder. She noticed some of the guests that had been in small singular same-sex groups were now beginning to mingle a bit more, echoing she thought the vicar's sentiments.

Several small groups were beginning to walk towards the bottom of the garden. It seemed that something exciting was taking place in the confines of the wild garden. There were giggles of excitement and cheery voices that were enticing others to follow them.

"Come on Mol, put down your tray" said the vicar taking the tray from her hands. "It seems we have fairies at the bottom of our garden."

In the distance Molly could see people jumping into the air, their arms raised clapping their hands together with each jump. Hands were snatching at something that was invisible to her. The vicar grabbed Molly's hand and pulled her towards him. Holding her hand, he started to skip towards the others, dragging Molly on behind. The commotion at the bottom of the garden had intensified.

As they got closer, Molly could hear shrieks of laughter and could see some of the ladies from the guild and the ministers skipping around waving their hands in the air. They were trying to catch what Molly could now see were dandelion clocks that had been blown from their stems.

"Isn't this wonderful, so many fairies" the vicar's wife called out to her. "See how many you can catch Molly."

Louise, seeing her husband, took his hand, severing it from Molly's. It was to the relief of Molly who walked quickly back to the top of the garden where Iris and Pru were watching the proceedings in total amazement.

"What the hell has got into them?" a very bewildered Iris asked.

"Better put the kettle back on Pru" instructed Molly politely. "I think some of the guests have been drinking too much wine."

Pru was dumbstruck. She did as she was asked, tutting under her breath as she went.

"It looks more like a vicar and tarts party," said Iris in a cynical but serious voice.

Molly thought she knew exactly what had caused this fiasco and whispered into Iris's ear. In response Iris burst out laughing.

Somehow the two trays of her fairy brownies that Molly had left on the side in her kitchen had been unintentionally brought along to the party. When Molly had left Iris and Pru in charge of packing up the food she had explained to Iris that the two trays set aside were not to be included. She had told her that they were her cakes that she had baked for Simon. Iris assuming that they were meant for a college event. Unfortunately believing that Iris was in control she had omitted to mention this to their willing helper for the day. She now realised that it must have been Pru. The two tray bakes of fairy brownies had been cut into small squares, packed, and unwittingly brought along to the vicar's party.

Molly knew she had no one else to blame but herself. She thought to herself that Pru must never find out about the mistake. Especially knowing that her husband was a retired police officer. The consequences of which she could only imagine.

Molly knew that Iris was trustworthy. She suggested to her that she could assist Pru in the kitchen making more tea and coffee.

Molly went across to the table. Her eyes scanning the remnants of the buffet. Discretely she gathered the remaining offending brownies from the plates. There were only three pieces left. These she put into a small plastic box and placed it into one of her bags.

She felt she had learnt a valuable lesson from this escapade. Never again she thought would she make her fairy brownies. Her good reputation might have been ruined if she had been found out. Molly decided she would destroy what remained of the weed when she got home that night.

"Think I might share the three brownies with Si though" she thought, smiling to herself. "Just for old time's sake."

After several more cups of tea and coffee were drunk, behavioural changes of everyone gradually became less raucous.

Happy guests took it in turns to approach the vicar and his wife to express their thanks and say goodbye as they began to depart. Some of the ladies showing signs of a more flirtatious behaviour. There was a lot of lingering hugs and kissing going on and not just by the vicar. All even hugged the caterers as they were leaving. Requesting a recipe here and there.

Pru was on cloud nine when the roman catholic minister took her hand and raised it to his lips to kiss it.

"I understand it is you I should thank for the excellent savoury pastries. I especially enjoyed the creamy ham and mushroom ones" he exclaimed.

As the last of the guests departed Molly and her team began the task of clearing up. The vicar and his wife were so appreciative of everything they had done in making the afternoon a success. The vicar followed Molly into the vicarage kitchen carrying a tray laden down with a mixture of crockery and leftover food. She turned and saw him just in time as it looked as if he were about to drop the tray.

"It's ok Vicar, you don't need to be doing this" said Molly, taking the tray from his hands.

With his hands now free and Molly having placed the tray on the work surface he took her into a bear hug, taking her by complete surprise, and proceeded to kiss her on both cheeks, lingering as he did so.

"I do wish you would call me Tom, Mol. You are a wonder to behold. What would I have done without you?" he whispered. "You and I would have made an excellent team" he said, kissing her ear.

Molly gently eased herself from the proximity with which she had found herself in but not before Iris witnessed the embrace. Iris guessed that the vicar had eaten more than one piece of brownie and that was the reason for his unholy behaviour towards Molly. She thought to herself that he would have a bad headache when he woke the next day and was not likely to remember his amorous behaviour. She also thought it was just as well that Louise had not witnessed the scene like she had.

Iris manoeuvred herself between Molly and the vicar and took his elbow.

"We are so pleased it went well for you vicar" she said, pushing him away as he made advances to her as well. "Now we really must get on with the clearing up. Got another busy day tomorrow you know" she concluded as she ushered him away, suggesting that he might like to have another cup of tea.

The vicar, on seeing Pru entering the kitchen door carrying another tray, proceeded to thank her equally amorously. Pru blushed terribly but seemed to enjoy the attention where Iris had been quite bemused by his actions. Molly grinned across at Iris catching her eye.

Only they knew the reason for the vicar's behaviour and for now would have to keep it to themselves.

Much later that evening over a bottle of wine Molly confessed to Simon and Rob what had happened to cause so much merriment at the tea party that afternoon.

"Best you give Iris the recipe. She could have a go at making them for us" Rob said jokingly before surprising Molly by adding that both he and Iris had dabbled in their youth.

"Of course, we only ever smoked the stuff, but I bet the brownies taste better."

Their evening ended when Rob thought it was time for him and Iris to leave. Molly took out one of the three pieces of brownie she had recovered from the party and gave it to Rob. "Enjoy for old time's sake" she whispered in his ear and kissed him on his cheek.

The Bells Are Ringing!

Chapter 1

As far as Molly was concerned, she had put the incident that had occurred at the vicar's tea party behind her and moved on. Save for a formal letter of thanks written on parish headed note paper Molly had had no further communication with the vicar. The last time she saw him was whilst on foot shopping in the village. Having noticed him on the other side of the road and before he could notice her, she entered the nearest shop door, tripping over a small step, only to find herself in the barber shop. The barber had very quick and managed to catch her just in time.

"Are you alright my dear?" he enquired, escorting her to the nearest chair. "Best you come and sit down for a minute."

A customer part way through having his hair cut saw the whole thing in his mirror.

"So sorry," said Molly. "I am fine. I just mistook your shop for the butchers. Was not concentrating where I was going. My age you know!" she said trying to make light of the situation.

Molly did however receive several more orders from some of the guests that had been at the vicar's party. Requests for her double chocolate brownies rocketed. The more traditional recipe would be adhered to in every order, Molly told herself.

Pru had been over the moon at being asked to help on that occasion and had secretly hoped that Molly would ask her again.

"Don't hesitate to ask me any time" she said when she had stopped Molly in the street whilst out shopping. "I did so enjoy helping you, and I know my sandwiches and pastries went down well. The vicar told me so, himself" she bragged.

Molly thought it highly unlikely that she would need to call on Pru in the immediate future but did not want to upset her. She had been immensely helpful. It really was not her fault that she had packed the fairy brownies by mistake.

"If anything comes up like that again Pru, you can be sure I will ask you. You truly are an amazing pastry chef." "And Pru's face beamed from ear to ear.

The British summer was well upon them. Sizzling hot days were followed by thunderstorms and torrential downpours. Molly had always referred to June and July as the months for weddings and in her business, it was a particularly busy time of the year. This July was to be no exception with three wedding cakes to be made as well as her orders of cupcakes to regular customers.

Iris was in her element. She had spent time over the previous weeks consulting with upcoming brides discussing their cakes and decorations.

Brides did not come alone as quite often they would bring along their partners and in some cases their mothers. For many, it was for support and guidance. However, in some instances diplomacy was called for when a mother had been overbearing and interfering. In these situations, Iris would turn her attention solely to the bride.

"It's really important that you put your own mark on the design of your cake to make it personal to you and your partner" she would say quite firmly.

Iris spent time sketching out their ideas. Tweaking them when she felt it would not work or look too ridiculous.

Molly was the baker when it came to baking larger cakes. She knew the best sponge recipes and shapes for baking that could be sculptured into designs that a bride had requested. Final decisions were only made after Iris and Molly had sat down and discussed the practicalities involved.

The fruit cakes for the up-and-coming weddings had been baked well in advance and left in airtight tins. Molly remembering to feed them with a little brandy now and again, adding to the rich flavour.

Many brides seem to have moved away from the traditional wedding cakes and opted for the more unusual. The three brides whose weddings were to be held in July were no exception.

Danielle and Marcus, whose wedding was the first of the three, had wanted to have a two-tier cake. One of chocolate and one of vanilla. Danielle's mother however had insisted it should have three tiers, with the bottom one being a fruit cake. She had got her own way and decorations for these cakes had been eventually finalised to everyone's satisfaction.

Tearful Helen, whose future husband, William, was a naval officer by profession, was still at sea. He was due home the week before the wedding having been at sea for two months. The arrangements for the big day had fallen to the bride and her family to organise. Helen's mother came across as a bit arrogant and intimidating. She had her own ideas when it came to the type of cake she thought her daughter should have and that it should be a fruit cake. There were heated differences of opinions between Helen and her mother. Iris was quick to realise that there might be a problem. Following the initial consultation with both the bride and her mother she arranged to meet Helen for a cup of coffee on her own. Helen not wanting to upset her mother had agreed to Iris's suggestion of a traditional fruit cake that could be decorated with naval symbols.

"The only problem is neither I nor Wills like fruit cake," said Helen. "We always said we would have a sponge cake, and I don't want Wills to be disappointed" she went on.

"Why not have two cakes then" Iris had suggested.

"Oh, could I? What a clever idea. Then I can have it decorated with pink rose buds just as we had planned. That is if you can do this?" she asked.

"We can do most things and rose buds are one of my favourite things to make" Iris responded reassuringly.

Two of the upcoming brides had been sorted.

The third bride was the most exciting of all. This was because the couple were friends of both Iris and Molly, and they would be attending the wedding itself. Jenny the bartender from the local pub had been dating Jack since January. They had got together and became sweethearts soon after the evening of the faggot burning. Friends closer to the couple had said they had been together long before this.

It was a phone call from Jenny asking if both she and Iris were free to meet her in the pub for a chat. No more details were forthcoming other than Jenny had exciting news to share with them. They agreed to meet on the Wednesday lunch time. A mutual day when both parties were free. Village gossip had rumoured that Jenny was expecting a baby because they were getting married so soon, but this had most definitely not been the case.

"I have always wanted to have a wedding of my own and I'm not getting any younger am I" said an excited Jenny taking a large bite from a thickly made ham and cheese sandwich. Some of its contents leaked out and dribbled down her chin falling into her lap. A dollop of Creamy white mayonnaise then dripped from the same sandwich onto the front of her blouse.

"Silly me, I am an arse" she said retrieving the larger crumbs and placing them back in her mouth before taking a second sandwich from the plateful that Sacha had made for them. She took an exceptionally large bite, and a similar spillage occurred. Molly wanted to take a napkin and mop her up but did not want to embarrass her.

There were no airs and graces where Jenny was concerned. What you saw is what you got. She was a simple sort of being. Happy, friendly, and tactile with everyone she knew. Everyone was fond of Jenny and that included Molly and Iris.

"Farmer George has offered us a cottage on the farm to live in. Jack can continue his work on the farm which he loves, and I can continue working here in the pub for Sacha and David. Mrs Brown said she could do with help with the farmhouse if I wanted some extra hours as well."

"I am so pleased for you Jenny. I must say I have noticed a twinkle in Jack's eye when he looks at you" Molly teased, causing Jenny to giggle.

"What sort of wedding are you planning?" asked Iris, wondering if they might be asked to make the cake.

"As you know I don't have any close kin, so we have asked Sacha and David to be our witnesses. They are so kind and have offered the pub as a venue, but we have other ideas. We are planning to have a church wedding and then a party in the old barn up at the farm" explained Jenny. "Farmer George offered it to us as a wedding present" she says excitedly. "And we have already spoken to Tom, and he is more than happy to wed us." Molly was surprised at Jenny's informality of using the vicar's first name.

"Sounds like you have it all organised. Please let us know if we can help in any way" Iris replies, offering her friend's help as well as her own.

"Oh, thank you," said Jenny getting up from her seat, leaning across the table to hug them both in turn. Molly took the first hug. Wet mayonnaise transferred from Jenny's blouse to Molly's new cream silk blouse that she had been wearing.

"Sorry Molly now look what I've gone and done. Here let me!" Before she could stop her Jenny picked up her soiled napkin and proceeded to wipe Molly's blouse resulting in an even larger greasy stain. "There you go Molly. Hardly notice it now."

Iris put her hand to her mouth to stifle a chuckle.

"I knew I could rely on you both. There is one thing I was going to ask you and that is will you be able to make a cake for us," said Jenny.

Molly and Iris looked at each and smiled. Molly, taking this to mean they were both in agreement, offered on their behalf to make the cake as a wedding gift. Jenny was over the moon!

"I know exactly what I would like" she continued as Molly took out a note pad and pen from her handbag.

"If it is possible, I would like a display of your cupcakes decorated with unicorns as well as a large cake."

Molly and Iris looked at each other blankly, neither knowing how to respond.

"If it's not possible I won't mind" Jenny continued noticing their hesitation.

Composing herself it was Iris who responded.

"We have never had a request for unicorns but:" she added smiling, "we do enjoy a challenge, so I am sure we can produce something for you. Can't we Mol?" And Molly agreed.

Molly had every confidence in Iris. She was the expert when it came to special requests like this. Molly felt sure that Iris would not have said they could do it, if it had not been possible.

So, it was agreed that Jenny would send them pictures of unicorns that she had collected. She explained to Molly and Iris how she had always had a fascination towards the mythical creatures.

"I know you will keep it a secret" Jenny lowered her voice and looked back over her shoulder making sure no one was eavesdropping before she continued.

"We want a fairy tale wedding! Not the Cinderella kind," she hastily added, "But one with proper fairies and such like."

Jenny continued to outline her own and Jack's ideas, sharing every detail. Molly and Iris listened as she prattled on excitedly.

And so it was that Jenny and Jack's wedding cake would be the most challenging yet for the baking duo.

Two days later Molly and Iris received the pictures of unicorns. Jenny had asked if the cakes could be of pastel rainbow colours.

"It's amazing what you can find on the internet" Iris said to Molly as she scanned for pictures on the computer.

Molly made them both a second cup of coffee and joined her friend at the computer.

"Look at this Mol" Iris said excitedly. "I think I have found the exact thing our Jen might be looking for. What do you think?"

The crafting company Iris had found said they could make edible pictures from drawings.

"I know I can sketch a head of a unicorn" she said confidently. "And then we can make the spiral horns ourselves."

"Wow! Iris, that sounds great."

"And I can sculp a large cake to give a three-dimensional effect with more unicorns."

There was still so much to consider. Not just with this cake but with all the cakes that were to be made during the warmer months of the summer. The risk of butter icing melting causing colourings to run could spoil any effect that they might have wanted to create. Edible wafer decorations could also have their own problems if icing were to become too soft. Wanting to alleviate any possibilities of this happening Molly decided to order six extra-large lined cool boxes for transporting the cakes.

Chapter 2

It was the third week into an unbearable hot July with daytime temperatures exceeding thirty degrees and dropping only slightly by night. The first two wedding cakes had been distributed a week apart to their destinations earlier in the month. The new cake boxes had been extremely useful.

Everyone had been delighted with the results. Helen's mother was so pleased with the naval decorated fruit cake that she immediately placed an order for another cake to be made to celebrate her own golden wedding anniversary later that year.

"I have lots of ideas and I do want it to be incredibly special, after all, fifty years of marriage is quite unusual these days" she had informed them in a dictatorial manner and sounding too confident.

"I will phone to make an appointment nearer the time" she concluded before turning her attention to a lady who was placing flower arrangements on the tables.

"Not there!" she shouted, startling the lady who almost dropped the vase she had been about to place on the pristine white tablecloth.

"We shall both look forward to seeing you then" Molly answered, retreating backwards as she spoke and holding her hands with crossed fingers behind her back so Iris could see that she had not really been truthful.

Back in Rosie and driving home they both started to giggle. Mimicking the lady's voice Molly turned to her friend and repeated what she had said.

"After all, fifty years of marriage is quite unusual these days."

"I pity her husband" Iris said, "I think I can guess who wears the trousers in that relationship."

Chapter 3

The day of Jenny and Jack's wedding had arrived. Earlier that morning Molly and Iris drove to the old barn where the reception was to take place. They had offered their services with the preparation and decoration of the reception venue. The medieval tithe barn with its magnificent oak timber beams was a popular events venue. Not just with locals but also the wider community. The barn which once belonged to the diocese was now owned by Farmer Brown. He had been responsible for the modernisation to ensure health and safety regulations could be adhered to, but this had not in any way detracted from the overall impressive structure of the building.

The vicar's wife Louise had taken on the preparation for the reception. She and Tom had got to know Jenny and Jack well. The previous vicar, her father-in-law, had been very fond of Jenny. When he retired, he had asked that his son and wife might look out for Jenny as she had no family.

The late vicar had explained to them that Jenny had spent her early years in a children's home. Jenny had known nothing of her birth parents and never felt the need to trace them. Her adoptive parents were from the parish. They had brought her up from the age of six and were the only parents she knew and had loved. Jenny was twenty-five when they passed away, just three months apart from each other, and she had been devastated. Their religious influence over her would continue as she made her own way in life.

Jenny had been left a small amount of money. The cottage had been a rental and Jenny was unable to keep up with the payments as her savings began to dwindle. She was overwhelmed when Sacha and David offered her accommodation in the pub. This could not have come at a better time for her.

Jenny was a willing helper. Anything that needed doing in the church she would volunteer to do. From cleaning to fundraising. She even managed to get herself roped in to help with the Sunday school. She had a natural rapport with young children.

Trestle tables and chairs had already been positioned in place and it was just the dressing of them needed. It was with Pat Brown, Jack's mother who took charge along with Louise that Molly and Iris set to and helped to decorate the tables and the room.

The tables were covered with pale pink and white paper cloths alternating with lilac and pale yellow. Bows of rainbow-coloured ribbons were tied to each chair. An assortment of jugs, glass jars and odd vases were filled with wildflowers and tall grasses. The vicar had generously donated these. Picked freshly that morning from the vicarage garden. Each one of the containers was decorated with even more ribbons.

At the far end of the room stood a separate table in position to receive the wedding cakes. The decoration similar but more elaborate than the other tables. Positioned in the centre of this table stood a tall cake stand made of wood fashioned to look like an old oak tree. The branches each with a fixed platform ready to hold the individual cupcakes. Jack had made it and Molly thought he had done a magnificent job.

Even with the barn doors open the room still felt too warm to put out the cakes. Molly and Iris had decided to make a swift exit after the service that afternoon and return to the barn to complete the tableau.

Molly had been putting final additions to some of the wall hangings when the vicar arrived. She had been standing halfway up the step ladder and was starting to come down when he noticed her.

"Molly my dear, you really should not be climbing ladders. Let me help you down" he insisted, raising his arms to catch her around the waist.

"Thank you, vicar, I can manage" she replied, causing him to frown as she wriggled out of his clutch stepping away from his proximity.

"Just popped in to see if I can help in any way but it looks like it has all been done. Lovely it all looks too" he said.

"Louise is over there, best check if she needs your help" said Molly pointing across the room to where Louise was now staring at her strait-laced.

"Hello dear" he shouted hurrying across the room to her side.

"That man!" said Iris who had witnessed the vicar's arrival and could see him advancing towards Molly. She had tried to wave and warn her friend of his approach but had been unsuccessful.

"It's all right Iris. I cannot help it if he fancies me" she said jokingly.

Molly had not told Iris anything about her connection with Tom other than that they had been friends at school. There were some things about him that she swore to keep to herself.

Satisfied that they were all finished, and all the decorating was complete, everyone left the barn to get ready for the service. The caterers had arrived as well as bar staff and musicians. Delicious smells wafted from the barbeque that was already lit. A whole pig was rotating on the rotisserie. One of the catering staff was basting the meat with a jug of liquid. As the contents encountered the meat it produced a sizzling sound and sent more tantalising aromas towards them.

"I'm looking forward to some of that," said Iris pretending to waft the smell to her nostrils.

"And me!" said Molly.

Molly and Iris were looking forward to what they thought and hoped would be the perfect wedding day for Jack and Jenny.

Chapter 4

There was not a cloud in the sky. It felt very warm. Intermittently an ever so slight breeze wafted by. Molly, as always, grateful for any resemblance of this.

Dressed in their wedding finery, Molly and Iris with their husbands took their seats in the pews.

"Bit cooler in here thank goodness" Molly remarked, fanning herself with her order of service.

"Not sure about the barn though" Iris responded.

All the wedding guests were local friends of both Jenny and Jack with a few relatives invited from the Brown family. Molly could not help herself from eavesdropping on a couple sitting in the pew in front of her. They both had strong west country accents.

"Isn't it a pretty church my dear!" said the woman.

"Arh! It is that my dear" came the reply.

"Do you remember our wedding in St Peters?"

"How can I forget my lovey! Twas the happiest day of my life so it was."

The man took his wife's hand and kissed it. Molly caught Iris's eye and knew that she had been listening to the couple too and they both smiled.

The church had been simply but beautifully decorated with more wildflowers and tall grasses. Each display having been tied in bunches with rainbow-coloured ribbons.

Jack arrived with his best man. Both identically dressed in country tweed jackets. Both wore open neck shirts with matching lilac-coloured cravats. As they entered the church, they removed their tweed caps. Molly thought how smart and different they appeared to the more usual groom attire. Although the church felt cool, Molly was concerned that even they might be a bit hot in the barn later.

As the organ struck the first notes of the familiar bridal march the formalities commenced. The bride on the arm of David, who was to give her away, looked beautiful but so different from any other bride Molly had seen.

She had been wearing a long length cream lace dress. It was fitted at the waist with a loose skirt. Around her waist she wore a green sash which tied into a large ribbon at her back. The hemline was jagged and the sleeves which came just below the elbow also had jagged edges. On the top of her head, she wore a circular headdress made of green leaves intertwined with multiple-coloured tiny wildflowers. In her hand she carried a mostly green leaved bouquet again with small flowers. She looked very nymph like.

Walking behind the bride came four small children. Two girls and two boys. All were wearing costumes made to look like fairy folk. All had headdresses of green leaves and carried baskets of flower petals. As they walked past her pew Molly could see attached to their backs, they all wore delicate see-through rainbow-coloured wings. They looked adorable.

"Bit old for that sort of dress, she looks ridiculous" Molly heard someone loudly whisper behind her. In response she turned and glared at the sour face of the speaker and the woman who had not realised she had spoken so loudly turned a crimson colour. How dare anyone cruelly criticise any bride for their choice of theme, Molly thought to herself. It was their special day, and they should be able to do whatever they liked even if it was a bit obscure and the bride being a little on the overweight size.

The service began with the hymn [All things bright and beautiful] which Molly thought had been most appropriately chosen by the couple for this occasion. The service went without a hitch save for the usual teasing from the best man who emptied all his pockets before producing the wedding rings, giving cause for the congregation to let out a little laughter.

The vicar's sentiments, Molly thought, had been almost exemplary. He had started by saying how he believed God had intended the couple to be together and that they were perfectly matched. He went on to say how like his father before him Jenny had given so much of her time to the parish. He said it was his privilege to be marrying them here in this church where they both worshipped regularly. Had Molly imagined that the vicar had briefly looked her way when he spoke those last words? He then went on to talk a bit about their attributes. Jenny's willingness to help others within the parish. He specifically referenced himself and his wife's gratitude for help with the little ones in the Sunday school. About Jack, he mentioned his voluntary work with the local scouts and his handy man jobs around the church. He also praised his talent in woodwork skills pointing out two commissioned pieces of woodwork in the church. One was a large, beautiful candle stand which Jack had made to replace an old one that had become beyond repair. The intrinsic carving detailing lit candles pointing up towards where the real candle would fit. The second piece would only come out at Christmas. A nativity stable complete with figurines and animals. It was exquisite.

"He's surpassed himself with that one" Molly whispered to Simon.

"Do you remember our wedding day Mol?"

"How can I ever forget? It was the best day ever" said Molly, smiling adoringly at her husband and taking his hand in hers. Again, a brief glance at the vicar and she thought she noticed him frown at her.

With the service concluded everyone proceeded to follow the wedding party out of the church. To everyone's delight there was a horse and cart waiting to take the bride and groom to the reception. I say, ???? it was The Horse's body that had been sprayed with pink patches and its tail had been sprayed in rainbow colours. The horse also had a coloured horn attached to its head. All this giving the appearance of a mystical unicorn.

"The poor beast" Molly overheard someone comment.

"Shouldn't be allowed" a reply came back.

This got Molly's back up and she glanced over her shoulder and scowled once again at the two women who had sat behind her in church. She wanted to say something to them but did not want to cause a fuss.

The rustic cart had been decorated with greenery and coloured ribbons. The young fairy children handed out their flower petals so everyone could throw them over the happy couple as Jack helped his wife into the cart before taking the horse's reins in preparation to drive them both slowly onto their reception. All those that could, walked behind them the short distance to the barn. Two of Jack's friends, one playing a whistle and the other a fiddle, led the procession playing the tune of [Marie's Wedding]. Those who knew the lyrics started to sing.

Step we gaily on we go.

Heel for heel and toe for toe.

Arm in arm and row on row.

All for Jenny's wedding.

And Molly joined in singing her heart out.

Whilst the first photographs were being taken outside the barn, Molly and Iris hurried on inside to put out the cakes. They were pleased with how they had turned out. The display looked amazing. They hoped Jenny and Jack would also think so. Simon had bought his camera to take photos of the wedding and the display of cakes for Molly's business.

With the formalities over including speeches and toasts Farmer Brown asked everyone to go outside for more photographs. The bride and groom had wanted a photo of everyone together outside with the barn behind them. Getting everyone together for this proved a bit of an ordeal for the photographer as he ushered people out making a shooing sort of sound. Many guests were tiddly by this time and were becoming noisy. Everyone had been given a glass of champagne to take outside with them. The idea being that they raise a toast in the air for the photograph.

"Has anyone seen my little fairies" Jenny called out, "must have them in the picture."

It took several minutes before someone located the four fairies and ushered them into position at the front of the group and minutes later the photograph was taken. The children ran off back to the barn. The photographer wanted to take a few more group photos before he was satisfied.

"One last thing to do" Jack shouted above the noisy guests. "We need everyone back inside to cut the cake."

Farmer Brown pushed forward and gave Jack an old knife from the house that he had cleaned up and tied ribbons to. Members of the Brown family had traditionally used it to cut their wedding cakes.

As everyone filed back inside, champagne glasses were topped up for a final toast. The bride and groom moved forward to assume their position by the table.

Molly and Iris, with their glasses refilled with champagne, also made their way forward. Everyone knew that they had designed and made the cakes. Blinking her eyes Molly looked towards the table. Something was amiss, she thought to herself. Jenny and Jack having reached the table gasped and turned towards Molly and Iris who were now hurrying towards them.

"Whoever would have done this?" a stunned Iris asked turning to Molly, who was in shock. She noticed beads of sweat on Molly's brow and that her face was turning very red.

"I am so sorry Jenny; I don't know who could have done such a cruel thing," said Molly.

The guests, who had been standing a little way back from the table, could not see what the problem had been and were waiting for the couple to cut the main cake. Their cameras at the ready.

Someone had removed all the unicorn horns from the cupcakes leaving small indentations in the icing.

With her eyes downcast Molly noticed four pairs of little ballet shoed feet sticking out from under the tablecloth. She raised the cloth a little higher to reveal all four giggling fairy children. Each had their flower basket. In the baskets were all the sugar horns that they had removed from the cakes. Jenny smiled before starting to laugh and Jack joined in. The rest of the guests, now understanding what had happened, also began to laugh.

"They are only children" Jenny said. "No harm really done is there our Jack" she continued before looking at Molly and Iris who were not seeing the funny side.

"Please don't worry you two!" said Jenny. "I'm sure someone will have photos of the before!" Hesitating and glancing around as cameras around the barn started clicking into action: "And lots more of the after!"

On seeing the bride and groom taking the incident so well everyone in the barn began to laugh.

"They're not fairies" Iris remarked to Molly crossly with a straight face causing Molly to be concerned. "We spent hours practising and making all those sugar horns. They are more like imps" she whispered in Molly's ear, and she began to smile.

Molly put her arm around Iris's shoulder giving her a gentle reassuring squeeze.

"Oh well! Guess this is another one, we won't be able to forget easily" said Molly smiling.

The large cake had been fortunately left intact. No impish behaviour here! Raising the knife Jack and Jenny made a cut. Both commenting on the softness of the pink and white marble effect sponge. They both took a piece to their mouths to sample, smiling and nodding their heads reassuringly at Molly and Iris. The remaining cakes were handed out to the guests.

Mr Kay shouted from the back: "Exceedingly good cakes Molly" creating a chorus of laughter.

"Light as a fairy" someone else shouted causing a more raucous sound that became infectious till everyone in the room was laughing.

A Big Birthday

50th

Chapter 1

Molly was never one for celebrating her birthday. This year was going to be particularly difficult as she was about to turn fifty. As was the same every year she made no attempt to remind anyone in her family or circle of friends of the upcoming event.

However, Simon was never one to forget her birthday and had always bought her gifts. Over the years she had built up quite a collection of ornamental giraffes. A display cabinet on the landing was now bursting with giraffes of all sizes and colours. Some made from wood and fabric whilst others were made from pottery and porcelain. Simon came to realise that enough was enough when she had hinted to him that they may need to buy another cabinet to house her collection.

Sometimes Simon chose gifts of a more personal nature. Like the time he had bought her a matching set of underwear. A silk bra and knickers which he presented to her on her fortieth. Despite being a very pretty set in a ruby red floral pattern and which had fitted her well, she was a little disappointed. She had teased him saying he had chosen the gift more for himself.

"I'll have you know your daughter chose them and they came from Paris" he told her, defending himself and making her feel guilty.

On her last birthday, celebrating forty-nine years, Simon exceeded himself. Molly had been overwhelmed with her gift of a spa day. This she had appreciated and had enjoyed the pampering which came with the deluxe package. It included a full body massage, a manicure and a facial.

In the evening Simon had taken her out for a splendid dinner to a small French restaurant where their speciality was seafood. She recorded this as being one of her best birthdays ever.

This year however Simon wanted to plan something even more special as it was her fiftieth birthday. He knew Molly did not want to celebrate because she had been feeling a bit down in the dumps of late. He also knew that her menopause was partly to blame for this. The absence of their daughter did not help either. It was unfortunate that Laura could not get over for the celebration.

However, he was determined not to let anything spoil the surprise which he had called on Rob and Iris to help with. He hoped it might cheer her up.

Molly was delighted with her gift of an afternoon tea for two with champagne.

"I want you to enjoy it with a friend" said Simon knowing full well that she would choose Iris.

"We can have a meal out any time to celebrate" he told her knowing he had more surprises up his sleeve.

"Bit short notice Si. Iris might have something else on" she said. "But I will ask her."

Simon had warned Iris, having predicted that Molly would invite her. Unbeknown to Molly at that time it was all part of a planned day of celebrations that Simon had organised.

Molly's birthday fell on a ridiculously hot and humid summer's day. The evening before the met office had put out a weather warning due to the extreme heat that were expecting. They had predicted that the heat wave could last for several days. This, Molly thought, was not good news as far as she was concerned.

Molly's menopause symptoms had been in full swing. She had been unable to concentrate on anything for any length of time. Poor Simon could not do anything right. Her mood swings had been intolerable. He had tried to be sympathetic towards her but in the end, he felt it easier keeping out of her way. The best way to do this was on the golf course. Molly found it necessary to change her clothes and take cool showers throughout the day just to cope. Sleeping at night had been the most difficult.

"Tossing and turning like that will just create more heat" Simon said, offering his advice. "Just try and lie still."

"You have no idea what it's like" she had replied before a full-blown argument between them had got out of hand, ending with her getting up and endeavouring to get some sleep in the guest bedroom. Neither of them was to get much sleep that night.

"Sorry Mol" said Simon apologetically when he had brought her mug of coffee the following morning.

"I'm sorry too" she had replied. "I just feel so tired and miserable."

"Perhaps it might be a good idea to see the doc just to see if there is anything else you can take" suggested Simon. "Only just till you are over the worst" he quickly added when he saw the expression on her face.

"I will give it some thought" she replied reassuringly, not wanting to upset him again. "I think the doctor might say I haven't given the HRT enough time yet."

Molly had not confided to Iris that she had decided to start HRT.

She had exhausted all other options. She was fed up swallowing tablet after tablet and bottle after bottle of herbal concoctions with no respite from her symptoms so had finally made the appointment, keeping it to herself. At first the new medication was working well.

The best birthday gift she had received had come from Iris. Molly removed the pretty wrapping paper to disclose a small plain box. There were no clues as to its contents.

"Here you are Mol, I forgot to give you the batteries to go with it."

"Oh! Iris, I hope it's not what I think it is, is it?" asked Molly grinning at her friend, and then the penny dropped. Iris burst out laughing.

"You don't think I would buy you one of those," Iris replied teasingly.

"Yes, knowing you as well as I do, I think you would" said Molly Jokingly.

"Best you open it and see, hadn't you, unless you want to save it till Si gets home."

Molly removed the sticky tape at one end of the box and peered inside. Still no clue. Sliding out an inner box onto her hand revealed its contents.

"Iris thank you. You could not have given me anything better and more useful than this," said Molly. "The best gift ever!"

Molly opened the end compartment and secured the batteries before turning on the handheld fan and wafted it over her face.

"It may not be my birthday Mol, but I bought one for myself as well" said Iris, taking a similar one out of her handbag." Much better than one of those other things. Wouldn't you agree?"

Molly gave Iris a huge hug. Together they held their fans under their chins.

"Sheer bliss!" They agreed.

Chapter 2

Molly and Iris were shown to their table, out on the terrace of the Palomino Hotel. There was a selection of small wrought iron tables for two and larger ones to seat more people. All had matching white chairs with cushions. Each table dressed in a pristine white linen tablecloth. Above them were opened floral sunshades. The vibrant yellow, orange, and blue spring flowered fabric matching those of the chair cushions. On the tables were small vases of flowers complementing the bright floral colour scheme.

The terrace overlooked the hotel gardens and had immaculately mown lawns with colourful flower borders. Trees and shrubs of various variety and sizes, mature ones as well as smaller ones, grew behind the flower beds. In the centre of the lawn was a patio area with the most amazing water feature displaying two white palomino horses standing on their hind legs with their front ones positioned so they looked as if they were dancing. Their tails plaited for the occasion.

"Eh! Mol, do you think they were originally unicorns, and someone removed their horns?" Iris joked, and Molly smiled.

"This is a bit good" Iris continued taking in the delightful surroundings. "Thanks so much for inviting me Mol."

"I knew you would like it" said Molly smiling at her friend. "I came once before with my mother to celebrate her birthday. That was some years ago though. It has new owners now and they have had the place completely redecorated."

"Very vintage! Don't you think? I love the colour scheme" said Iris, picking up an edge of the tablecloth to feel the material between her fingers. "Good quality! Molly agreed.

When the waiter returned to their table, both requested tea as their choice of beverage.

"I really have to cut down on my coffee intake" said Molly, who noticed Iris's surprised face.

A second, younger and more handsome waiter in a pristine uniform returned to their table pushing a tea trolly. He placed a floral decorated vintage teapot of steaming tea onto the table with matching plates, cups and saucers, milk jug and a sugar bowl. He then placed a three-tier stand on the table containing a selection of very tiny sandwiches and savoury pastries. On a separate plate were two exceptionally large scones with bowls of strawberry jam and clotted cream. Across the table Molly smiled at Iris whose mouth was slightly agape with surprise.

"Enjoy" said the waiter, smiling. "Let me know if you require more hot water for the tea … or anything else." With what the women thought had a distinctive undertone.

"Thank you" they replied simultaneously.

They munched their way through the selection of sandwiches and pastries each commenting on their favourite fillings. Next, they ate a scone each with large helpings of jam and larger amounts of clotted cream.

"Just cannot help myself! I just adore clotted cream" said Iris as she took a bite, not aware of the smudge of cream left on her nose.

Molly grinned and, touching her own nose, made Iris aware and she picked up her napkin from her lap to wipe it away. Embarrassed Iris, grinning, looked around to see if anyone had noticed.

 Expecting to end with a slice of cake and a glass of champagne they had been surprised when the waiter returned with another, more ornate three-tier cake stand full of an assortment of small, delicate cakes and a bottle of champagne with two glasses.

"Wow!" exclaimed Iris loudly so everyone else on the terrace could not help but overhear. "This must have cost your Simon a packet."

"I'm stuffed already," said Molly. "Not sure if I can eat any of the cake" she said, rubbing her hand over her full stomach.

"Not going to do much for my diet" Iris chipped in.

They both laughed aloud causing one or two people to stare at them with straight faces.

"I don't care" Molly said. "They can think what they like. It's my birthday and I am determined to make the most of it."

Iris raised her glass to wish Molly a happy birthday for the second time that day.

Sipping their cold champagne, they both tucked into some of the cakes. Each choosing different pieces and then sharing them so that they could both taste and comment on texture and flavour. Their voices becoming a little louder.

"That lady over there keeps staring at us" Iris said, using her eyes to point Molly in the direction of a couple seated at a table opposite to them.

"Perhaps she thinks we are professional critics" Molly said chuckling, taking out a pad of paper and pen from her handbag which she always carried and then pretending to take notes as they continued sampling small bites from every cake on the stand.

The cold champagne had tasted delicious. Consuming alcohol in the middle of the afternoon and on one of the hottest days of the year so far was not such a clever idea.

"I'm feeling a bit squiffy and lightheaded" said Iris, taking another small cake from the top tier which then slipped from her hand, landing upside down on her plate and causing her to giggle.

"And what do we think of the texture of this little cake?" asked Iris in a voice loud enough for the couple to hear, as she turned the cake over revealing a soft gooey mess of butter cream. Iris divided the already small cake in two halves and transferred one piece onto Molly's plate.

"Don't think we can blame the chef for this one" replied Molly, lifting a fork of cake to her mouth. "It's exceedingly difficult with butter icing in this sort of weather" she said in an exaggerated posh voice.

The play-acting went on till they were both giggling so much they had to stop. They decided they should order some more tea to help sober them up.

"I think I will have a coffee this time," said Molly.

"Perhaps I better join you," said Iris.

The couple opposite had finished their tea and were making a move to leave the table. As they walked past them the lady gave them a look of disapproval which only caused Iris to start giggling again.

The waiter returned with his trolley. He transferred the tray which held a jug of coffee and clean cups and saucers onto their table. Lifting the trolley cloth, he took out two tall sundae glasses filled with trifle and topped with fresh strawberries. For the first time that afternoon both women were speechless and just sat staring at each other. The waiter smiled knowing that the dessert, as he found with most customers, were not expected.

"These are a new addition to our afternoon package. They are exceptionally light and cooling so I hope you will enjoy them, especially on such a sweltering day" he said, placing new napkins and long-handled spoons in front of them.

The two women tucked into their desserts.

"Wow!" remarked Iris. "This is delicious."

"Best trifle I have ever tasted" stated Molly. "And I have eaten more than a few in my time."

It had been arranged for Rob to collect the ladies and take them home after they had finished their afternoon tea. It was Iris who made the call informing him that they had finished tea and were ready to be picked up from the hotel.

"I trust you had a good time" he asked them as he helped the giggling pair into their seats.

"Thanks Rob it was a real treat," said Iris.

To Molly: "Thank you for inviting me." And Molly lightly squeezed Iris's hand.

"I don't think I will be able to eat anything for a week at least" said Molly. "I'm so stuffed and I think I might need a lie-down when I get home."

Rob caught Iris's eye in the rear-view mirror and winked at her and Molly noticed this and smiled to herself.

Iris responded by returning a wink and smiled back at him. A thought then suddenly occurred to her. Had Rob been winking as a secretive reminder of the fact that the birthday celebrations were not yet over for Molly or had the wink meant something else? Iris blushed at the thought and once again noticed Rob was smiling at her in the mirror.

"I'm glad you both enjoyed yourselves" he said.

Molly was relieved to get home. Heading straight for the bathroom where she hurriedly stripped off her sweaty damp clothes. She stepped into the shower and immediately turned down the water temperature until it was barely warm. The cool water was just what Molly needed. The perfect end to a perfect afternoon.

"Just a little nap" she thought to herself. The alcohol still influencing her tiredness. Molly did not think it necessary to dress again so chose to put on a light silky dressing gown before pulling the blinds, closing the curtains, and curling up on the bed. She knew that later that evening she and Simon had made plans to have a quiet evening in front of the television. Simon had suggested they have a takeaway and a bottle of wine and that he would organise it.

"Sheer bliss" a contented Molly said aloud before she fell into a deep sleep.

Chapter 3

Simon returned home later that afternoon and found Molly lying on the bed. The curtains were pulled together, keeping out the bright sunshine that was still very much prominent for late afternoon. The windows were open, letting in a warm breeze causing the curtains to flutter. On hearing Simon entering the room Molly began to arouse, stretching her body in an enticing way and sighing as she did so. Her wrap-around gown became loosened as she moved revealing her nudity underneath. The silk material parting at the neck revealing the soft contours of her breasts.

Simon was becoming very turned on by her continuous erotic stretching.

"Hi Si" Molly whispered as he came to her side. "I think the champagne went to my head more than usual, I think it must be the heat."

"Mind if I join you birthday girl" he asked, not waiting for a reply, and hurriedly removed his clothes. Simon thought his Molly was still incredibly attractive for fifty and he still found her very sexy.

After making love they lay quietly together. Molly resting in the crook of Simon's arm.

"Simply the best birthday ever" she said smiling and offering up her lips for more kissing.

Then without any warning Molly suddenly became uncontrollably hot, sweaty, and moved quickly away from his body contact. Reaching out to the bedside table she picked up the small fan that Iris had given her and switched it on. Positioning it firstly over her face and neck before fanning herself across her chest and down to her thighs where they were sticking together from sweat.

"That was a horrible one" says Molly as the anxious and hot feeling begins to subside.

"Poor you Moll, I wish I could do something to help" says Simon, pulling her back into his arms.

"I think just loving me and putting up with me will help me get through, however long it takes" she said smiling as she remembered the tiff they had the day before.

It had been over something quite silly really. Molly had accused him of tidying away some important paperwork relating to a client she had met earlier that day. Specific instructions for delivering a surprise celebration cake. The address had been one she had not been to before and her client had wanted the cake to be delivered to the back door where caterers would be waiting for her at a designated time. It was only when she had gone to a drawer in her desk that she had found the papers and instantly remembered she had put them there herself. Molly hoped that her sometimes occasional forgetfulness was linked to her menopause symptoms and that things would eventually improve. Something she knew she needed to find out.

Simon would never know how many times during the balmy and sometimes sweltering hot nights that Molly would get up and sponge herself down with cool water. There were times now when Molly had believed herself to be less attractive to Simon. She worried that she might smell sweaty and unclean. She would change the bedsheets more frequently. He recently commented that he thought she had changed them just the day before and Molly had felt embarrassed.

Molly now changed the bed linen while Simon was at work.

"Hope you don't mind Mol, but I reconsidered. I have booked a table at the pub for a meal tonight. It just did not seem right having a takeaway on such a special birthday."

"I am glad I took a nap then. Not sure I would have wanted to go out otherwise" she replied.

"I've booked for 8 o'clock, hope that's ok" he says.

"Better get up and doll myself up then" she says with a sigh pushing away the bed sheet and making to get up.

"Plenty of time for that" says Simon pulling her back into his arms.

"Will possibly need to fake this one" she thought, pulling the sheet back over their entwined bodies.

They both showered and dressed for the evening's occasion. While they waited for their taxi that Simon had arranged, he opened a bottle of champagne.

"Here's to you Mol" he said, charging his glass and then kissing her on her freshly painted lips. "Happy birthday my love" he toasted.

Having made making love twice that afternoon had given Molly a little more of an appetite.

"Perhaps I could just manage a starter" she suggested to Simon who smiled at her without verbally responding. He knew Molly would have an appetite of a horse after sex.

The taxi pulled up outside Old Harry's Arms and the pair got out. Molly waited while Simon spoke to the driver, confirming the pickup time for the return journey. She was a little disappointed when he suggested midnight. The two glasses of champagne they had drunk while waiting for the taxi was making her feel tired again and she hoped they would eat quickly and get home. Hopefully finishing the evening with a film and a small liqueur as well as plenty of strong coffee.

"Don't want to rush it" said Simon as he took her arm, ushering her towards the door.

No one could have been more genuinely surprised when the door opened, and a loud chorus of Happy Birthday greetings were heralded towards them. Molly was genuinely dumbfounded and honestly a little disappointed.

The first to greet them were Rob and Iris, who she realised must have been in on it the whole time. Molly turned to Simon with a straight face. Kissing him on the cheek she whispered into his ear.

"You know I don't like birthday party surprises" she said before turning round and forcing a smile towards her friends.

Iris thought she saw the disappointment in her friend's face.

"Come on Mol" she says, "it wasn't really all Si's fault, we all encouraged him to do this."

There was nothing that Molly could do now but make the best of it. Iris took Molly by the hand and gave it a squeeze as she led her into the crowded room.

"I was rather looking forward to a quiet meal for two" whispered Molly.

"You obviously haven't noticed the buffet over there yet" Iris responded pointing towards the tables laden with food at the far end of the room.

"You have Pru to thank for that. Si asked her if she would organise everything to give us both a day off and she did not hesitate."

Pru hurried forward to join them when she saw Iris pointing towards the buffet tables. She had just been adding the final garnish to the trays of food to complete what she had hoped would appear to be a professional job.

"I hope you will approve Molly" she said, taking her hand from Iris's clasp and escorting her closer to the tables. "I have made lots of things that I hope you will like. I did check with Simon and Iris for suggestions as well."

"Pru it all looks so delicious, you have done a wonderful job, thank you." Molly gives Pru a kiss on her cheek and Pru's face beamed.

In the centre of the table stood an incredibly beautiful birthday cake. The decorations included small yellow roses and matching ribbons. The centre of the cake had been made to look like a pond. In its centre was an exquisite sugar-moulded swan. Not wanting to spoil the effect, Iris had placed a fiftieth candle on a stand next to the cake itself. Molly turned towards Iris smiling. She knew there was only one person who could make a cake like this. The sentiments of the swan were special too and Molly thought Iris clever to remember this.

Iris, remembering the vicar's tea party and the short notice Molly had been given to prepare for it, had observed her as she worked in the kitchen.

"Mol" she had asked, "why are you always so calm and collected?"

"Iris" she replied, "I'm like a swan, calm and graceful on the surface but paddling madly under the surface."

"Thank you so much Iris, the cake is so beautiful" she said, giving her a hug and fighting back emotional tears.

"Don't you go crying today," said Iris. "It's bad luck to cry on one's birthday" she teased.

David and Sacha had closed the pub for the evening due to the private function being held in honour of Molly. This did not really matter as most of the guests at the party were locals anyway. A few business associates as well as friends from Molly's youth had also been included.

Molly began to relax as various people greeted her. Hugs and kisses were certainly in great supply. Everyone keen to remind her of the time when they had first met and what they had got up to. Some embarrassing stories relayed to her that she had hoped had been long forgotten.

"Do you remember when...?" and "Oh! You cannot have forgotten how we ...." were echoed around the room. There had even been one or two whispered mentions of the infamous chocolate brownies.

After her second glass of red wine Molly really began to let herself go and joined friends on the dance floor or [at least an area created to be a dance floor] where would- be tables had been stacked away to make space. She had even forgiven Simon, dragging him on the floor to dance with her against his will.

Jack, who had returned from his honeymoon, had supplied the recorded disco dance music from the seventies and eighties.

Later into the evening the tempo changed to a slower pace allowing couples to smooch around the dance floor. This time it was Simon who sought Molly out and took her onto the floor to dance.

"You look as if you are enjoying yourself" he said to her as she relaxed against him, putting her arms around his neck.

"I am" she replied. "Talking with some of my old friends has made me realise how lucky and happy I am" she told him. "Do you know how many of our friends are on their second husbands or even their third?" she said smiling and nuzzling into his neck where his cologne wafted into her nostrils.

"Wouldn't change you for anyone here" he teased, whispering into her ear, and reminding her of what they had been up to earlier.

"I have one more birthday surprise for you my love" he told her.

"Think I had that one earlier" she said playfully.

"You will have to wait till tomorrow for the last surprise" Simon told her. "I know you will like it."

The party had gone well. She had cut the cake, and everyone sang happy birthday to her, threatening teasingly to give her fifty bumps. Steadying herself by placing her hands in front of her on the table for support she made a short, slurred speech thanking everyone who had helped and to her guests for coming. She truthfully told them all how she had felt overwhelmed.

"You all know how I hate being the centre of attention and celebrating my birthday is no exception, especially this one" she said as she began to sway a little from side to side as the feeling of intoxication began to take its effect on her.

Everyone began to clap and cheer. Simon hastens to her side.

"Anyway" she went on. "Enjoy the rest of the food and I have just been told its last orders at the bar but no more for me I think."

Molly had often drunk a little too much alcohol rendering her a little tipsy, but she knew when she had to stop.

Simon took Molly's arm through his own leading her onto the dance floor for their final smooch.

"Thanks Si I do feel a bit tiddly and tired. Do you think we can go home now?"

"Good idea" he told her. "Taxi should be here shortly. Let's slip out quickly while most people are at the bar."

Iris saw what they were planning and hurried across the room to give her friends a final hug.

"Hope you have enjoyed yourself Mol and that you will forgive the secrecy. It has been such a busy day for you. I will see everything is cleaned up so don't worry about a thing" she said, squeezing Molly more tightly than usual.

"Thanks Iris you are one in a million. I really have enjoyed myself. The entire day had been such fun, but I cannot wait any longer to get to bed," the last phrase being said more loudly, and just as the last song had finished and the room had become less noisy.

Everyone turned around and jeered at the couple as they left the room calling out suggestions to them both about what to do and what not to do when they got to bed.

Chapter 4

Molly slept far more than her usual six hours. She had been dead to the world for a good eight uninterrupted hours. Not one hot flush. At least that she could remember. Simon had been up a little while. He had one more surprise for his wife and was as excited as he hoped she would be. Molly drank two full mugs of coffee and had swallowed two paracetamol tablets before she felt ready to get up. Simon had instructed her to shower and dress as he was keen for her to receive her gift.

An hour later and after she had eaten two slices of toast and drank a further mug of coffee there was a knock at the door.

"It's ok Mol I'll get it" shouted Simon from the hallway where he had been hanging around pacing the hall floor for at least the last ten minutes.

Molly was more than a little stunned when she was handed her gift. This was most definitely not something she had ever asked or wished for. It was the last thing she had expected and the last thing she had ever wanted. The timing of this gift could not have come at a worse time. As far as Molly was concerned there never would have been a right time.

As she stood motionless and unable to speak, Simon placed the small black furry creature into her arms. It began to whimper and squirm in her arms and began licking her face and neck. The nervous but adorable creature then decided to relieve itself. The warm wee dribbling over her hands and down the front of her clean clothes. Molly stood still as if traumatised and in shock and handed the puppy back to Simon.

"It's alright" he says, "I'll sort it."

"You bet you will" she says glancing down at her blouse and trousers soaked in pee.

"Don't be cross Mol, he couldn't help, it's just a bit overwhelmed I expect."

"Me too!" says Molly.

It had been Simon that had always wanted them to have a dog, not she.

It had been Simon who had said that a dog would fit into their life easily, not her.

It had been Simon who had begged her on many occasions to consider having one.

It had been Simon who insisted he would take charge of walking and feeding it if they had one.

And it was Molly who had eventually given in. She said she would seriously give some thought to it but was not aware she had done this.

"Oh yes it will be Simon who would have to sort it" she said sarcastically but sweetly to him.

Chapter 5

Molly and Simon had usually planned their summer holiday for the end of August. With the college closed at this time was one reason for this. This year however, they had decided not to go away as they had hoped to go to France later in the year and spend time with their daughter Laura.

The last two weeks of August was turning out to be one of the wettest on record. It took Molly the first few days to get over the shock of the new puppy. During this time, she had given Simon the silent treatment after letting him know how she had felt.

"I just wish you had discussed it with me first" she had told him.

"If you remember we did talk about it, and I thought you were coming around to the idea" Simon responded on the defensive.

"Just because I said I would think about it, it didn't mean I had agreed to have one" Molly retorted just as the small puppy jumped up onto her lap without any warning, knocking the glass of red wine from her hand and spilling the contents all over the tired cream carpeted floor of the lounge.

"That's just great!" said Molly flippantly. "I was only saying last week that we needed to look at getting a new carpet. I think we had better wait a few more months. Give us time to get used to the idea of him running around."

Simon was quick to respond, running into the kitchen and bring back a bucket containing a cloth and the bottle of carpet spray that never seemed to get put away anymore. The bucket now having a permanent home down by the side of the kitchen unit for easy access. It had been useful too many times to count.

"How big do you think it will grow" asks Molly as she was playing a tug of war game with the puppy.

"The breeders said both parents were quite small. I did see the bitch and she was only medium in height. She had a lovely temperament too!"

"That is something I suppose! I am not sure I could have coped with a bigger dog."

The puppy began to tire and eventually settled down to sleep in its new bed. Molly smiled and bent down to stroke it. Simon noticed how Molly was bonding with their new pet and although not out of the doghouse yet, he believed everything would eventually settle down. And he was glad.

While Molly and Simon stayed home with their new addition to their family, their best friends were spending two sunny weeks in Spain with their own family and Molly had felt a bit envious of the couple. Her jealousy was only made worse by the continuous excessive rain that had fallen at home day after day. When the sun had decided to shine, and the temperature went up with humidity it created thunderstorms. Down would come torrential rain again and on one occasion they experienced some of the largest hailstones they had ever encountered. This was Vanda's first encounter of a storm such as this. Following the first loud clap of thunder he ran across the room with his tail between his legs and crawled on his belly taking refuge under one of the pair of low couches in the lounge. Neither Simon nor Molly could encourage him out. Eventually they would have to move the heavy piece of furniture to retrieve him. He was so frightened by this, and Molly felt sorry for him. She picked him up and wrapped him in her cardigan. Holding him close she comforted him and kissed his head. Simon observed her, smiling to himself.

With Iris away Molly managed the baking on her own. There had only been the regular customers to deal with as they had both agreed not to take on any extra orders for the last two weeks of the month.

Simon, with time on his hands, concentrated on vital puppy training.

An Inspector Calls

Chapter 1

Simon returned to work at the beginning of September leaving Molly to cope with their new puppy as well as running her business.

Molly was grateful that Iris was now home after her grandparent duties (as she always referred to it!) Having on this occasion accompanied their family to Spain for two weeks.

"Rob and I love helping with the little ones during the summer holidays but this time it was quite exhausting especially with the traveling as well. Our age! Think we need a holiday to get over it!"

"Well, it's lovely to have you back and I must say you look quite refreshed considering" said Molly, feeling a little envious of Iris's time spent with her family.

"It is good to be home, and I am really looking forward to getting back to work in your kitchen. A change is as good as a rest, so they say!"

A refreshed and Mediterranean-bronzed looking Iris had taken to the puppy far more positively than Molly initially had. She made a great fuss of the bundle of fur. Speaking to it as one would talk to a small child. She was a natural. The puppy rolled from its front to its back lapping up the attention.

"What are you going to call him?" asked Iris as she let the little pup climb all over her and the couch she had been sitting on with its newly frayed edge at the seams. It had not taken long for the puppy to start chewing everything in sight. Its claws catching on the fabric of the couch and pulling out strands of cotton.

"Vanda" answered Molly decisively. "As in vandalism. He is chewing everything. Even had a pair of Si's trainers the other day. You know the new ones he bought quite recently. I know I shouldn't have but I could not stop laughing."

"Well, that's what puppies do, isn't it Vanda?" said Iris, making a fuss of the puppy. "He is gorgeous, aren't you" to the puppy. "If you ever need someone to look after him Mol you can count on us. You know, holidays and things."

"Thanks Iris that's really kind. Not sure even Si has really thought of the implications" replied Molly.

Molly went on to tell Iris how Vanda had become quickly obsessed by the mail delivered through their letter box.

"All in all, I think it's an appropriate name isn't it boy?" said Molly, fussing the dog as it sought her attention by rolling onto his back.

Vanda, who by now was beginning to get sleepy having kept its owners up for most of the night, left Iris's lap and went to its bed.

Leaving the lounge and carrying the bed with the sleeping pup Molly and Iris moved to the kitchen where Molly made them both a coffee. They sat down at the kitchen table and started to make plans for the September orders. Vanda was always happy to sleep in the warmth of the kitchen. He did not like being left on his own in the lounge when others were in the kitchen.

As well as the regulars they had two more wedding cakes to decorate and three other celebration sponge cakes to design and make. One being a retirement cake, the second an anniversary and the third was for a fortieth birthday surprise.

It had been while they were deep in conversation drinking their second mug of coffee and discussing their work schedule that the postman had called. Both were too engrossed and excited with their plans to notice that Vanda had heard the post box clatter and had left his bed to investigate the sound as he had on every occasion since he had moved in.

It was just the day before when there had only been one envelope pushed through the letter box and Vanda had managed to retrieve it before it had landed on the floor. He had pulled at it as it was being posted through the aperture. Kevin their postman, thought this was very clever indeed. Simon, who had been preparing to go to work, had seen Kevin from an upstairs window. Having delivered their mail, he watched as Kevin walked back down the path. He wanted to check that he would close the gate behind him. The new sign (NEW DOG please shut the gate) Simon had only nailed to the gate the day before. He was just making sure that Kevin had acknowledged it.

Suddenly remembering what had happened the days preceding this one, he hurried back down the stairs. Only just in time to remove the dog-eared and slobbered-on letter from Vanda's teeth before it could be ripped to shreds. His next job, he then decided, was to fix a basket to the letter box so that the mail could fall safely into it. That would have to wait until the weekend though.

With Vanda safely asleep in her bed, or so they had thought, the women decided to check their stock and prepare Moly's office for the following day when baking would commence.

It was only after this that Iris left through the back door and Molly went to check on the puppy. He was still curled up and sound asleep. He was making a sort of snoring noise and Molly thought he looked quite adorable. She bent down and stroked the sleeping puppy.

"You sound just like your daddy" she said to him. Vanda opened his eyes, responding to the soft voice and the hand that had been stroking her. He licked the hand before rolling over and going back to sleep.

"Mustn't let daddy know I'm growing quite fond of you" she whispered in the little puppy's ear.

Leaving Vanda asleep in his bed, Molly- with a fresh mug of coffee- went to walk through the hallway and into the lounge. She had hoped to put her feet up and read the newspaper and then to rest her eyes for a few minutes.

How had Vanda managed to creep out of the kitchen without herself and Iris noticing him? Remnants of that morning's post was strewn across the hall floor.

"Damn Simon" she shouted aloud, waking the sleeping puppy who came to see what all the fuss was about. With his tail wagging it sidled up to her. Sitting at her feet he waited for the usual petting he had come to expect.

"You naughty boy!" Molly shouted, wagging her finger at the dog. "How many times have we told you no!" she said.

Molly was furious. More so at Simon who had promised to fit a basket to the letter box. Vanda, who did not understand the reason for the elevated voice and had yet to learn the different tones, just wanted to play. He started to grab at Molly's socked toes for attention before running circles around the hall and into the lounge. Repeating the movement as if on an assault course.

"Oh no you don't" she said catching him just as he had completed the fourth run around her feet. "it's back in the kitchen for you." She placed the puppy in its bed and very firmly told him to stay. Vanda did what he thought was expected of him but still his tail continued to wag. Just in case it had been a game.

Closing the door behind her Molly retrieved the mishmash of tattered paper, carrying the two handfuls into the lounge.

From the kitchen came whimpering sounds followed by scratching at the door which Molly chose to ignore.

On her knees she cleared the coffee table of its clutter and began trying to sort the pieces of paper. Having first deciphered what had been envelopes and putting these to one side she attempted to sort the letters. Some of the wording had become illegible due to the puppy's slobbering. As if that was not enough, there seemed to be words completely missing. She could only assume that the dog had eaten these. She only hoped that the pieces would pass through its digestive tract and present itself in the appropriate manner. Putting aside all what she thought appeared to be pieces of jargon she started to sort the important ones. Anything that had been addressed to Simon, she put into a separate pile. "He can have the privilege of sorting that lot" she said aloud. Molly began taking each piece of the remaining bits of paper as if she were doing small jigsaw puzzles. Slowly bit by bit she began to make out some of the mail.

There had been two thank-you letters from appreciative clients, and these helped to change Molly's mood from one of anger to one of short-term smugness.

She put the letter from Revenue & Customs reminding her to complete her tax return forms to one side.

The next letter was an invoice from one of her suppliers. She could not be sure how much she owed as the piece of paper totalling the amount at the bottom of the page was missing. She made a note to phone them later.

A letter containing a cheque from the bakery for their previous month's order was in several bits and she would have to request another one before she could bank this.

The last letter and the one that had taken her by complete surprise giving cause to put her in a flustered state and rendering a hot flush had come from the local council. She was to expect a visit from the safe food and hygiene inspection office and the date for the visit had been on this day. Sometime during that afternoon to be precise.

It had been fortunate that she and Iris had already spent time that morning cleaning, prepping, and checking stock. Still, she would need Iris to be there as she was her employee.

There was no time for lunch. A quick panicking phone call to her friend and Iris was by her side.

"Calm down Mol and remember the swan" Iris said encouragingly and watched as Molly took in a few deep breaths. "I'm sure it's just a routine inspection but I am surprised they haven't given us more warning."

Iris could always be called upon to calm a situation.

"Just hoping no one had made a complaint against us," said Molly.

198 | MOLLY MUNDAY'S CUPCAKES

"That's most unlikely, now isn't it" replied Iris smiling. "We are always so careful and professional, never seen a cleaner kitchen than your office."

A ring on the doorbell set Vanda off barking and scampering towards the hallway.

"Deep breaths Mol," said Iris. "It'll be ok you'll see."

Iris picked up the continuously yapping Vanda and accompanied Molly as she went to open the door. With one last deep breath and with an engaging smile Molly opened the door. Neither of them was prepared for who had been on the other side of it. Two official looking inspectors carrying briefcases.

"Good afternoon, my name is Susan Jameson, and this is my associate, Miles Faulkner. You are expecting us."

Molly had difficulty gaining her composure. Not because they were here but because they were no other than the couple who had been seated opposite them at the Palomino hotel on the day of her birthday celebration outing. Susan Jameson extended a handshake, but Miles Faulkner did not.

"Please come in" invited Molly. "Please excuse our new puppy." Vanda had made up his mind to dislike the visitors straight away and was yapping noisily. Molly thought that he was aware of her nervous vibes. Iris took immediate control of him by picking him up.

Entering the hallway, and in that moment when the inspectors' backs were turned on them, Molly took a second to glance at her friend and could see she was equally shocked, as she too had recognised the couple. However, the inspectors had not recognised them. Not yet anyway, Molly thought to herself, gaining her composure, and remembering the swan.

The small entourage moved from the hallway into the kitchen and then through to Molly's office. Iris stopping briefly to place the puppy onto its bed. Firmly telling him to stay.

"What a lovely work area you have for your business Molly," she said. "May I call you Molly?" she asked politely. "It's strange but you do look a bit familiar to me" she said smilingly towards her. Molly smiled nonchalantly towards her as if dismissing this as unlikely.

Miles Faulkner was to be a more forbidding character and so far, had been unable to show any warmth towards them, not even a smile. He placed his briefcase on the work bench and proceeded to take out a large black folder. From inside his jacket pocket, he took out a pen and proceeded to date an official piece of headed paper.

"This is just a formality and there's no need to worry" said Susan to Molly, seeing that she was looking flushed in the face. Susan had learnt throughout her career that many people who had these sorts of inspections were nervous. It was the serious nature of her job to ensure public safety but that did not mean she had to be unpleasant unless, of course, she was to find something so inappropriate or dangerous when she had the authority to enforce action on the owner and their work premises.

Molly had always been meticulous with both hygiene and safety within her workplace.

Susan Jameson appeared to be the one in charge as she was the only one speaking whilst Mr Faulkner, with little or no eye contact with them, continued to make notes.

"Molly, please can you show me a copy of your safer food, better business diary" Susan Jameson asks kindly, taking out a pair of spectacles from her handbag.

"Yes of course," says Molly as she moves towards her laptop on the desk.

Calmly and efficiently, Molly downloads the information that they had requested. She offered them both chairs that they may sit. They declined. The two inspectors browsed over the documentation.

"Can I offer you a cup of tea or coffee perhaps" says Molly, thinking if she made one for them then she could also have one for herself.

"That's kind but no thank you" said Miles Faulkner, speaking for the first time and for both.

Molly looked towards Iris and raised her eyebrows. She mouthed silently (Good cop, Bad cop) to which Iris responded with a nod.

Having inspected the documentation, they then requested to check the cupboards. With clip boards and pens they proceeded to open cupboard doors, checking the interiors and the contents. Susan Jameson made notes whilst Miles Faulkner completed what was a series of multiple-choice questions where ticks and crosses were all that was required.

Once they had done this, they moved towards the ovens. Molly and Iris stood the short distance away at the work bench watching them as the couple continued their inspection. They were talking to each other quietly, so it was sometimes difficult for Molly and Iris to hear what they had been saying. All the while they were taking notes. It was when they had moved across the room to the sinks and started looking into the cupboards underneath that Iris noticed the door beginning to open and the puppy creeping in. Vanda quickly moved towards its owner wagging his tail.

Without any warning it bent its back legs and proceeded to wee on the floor. As if this was not enough it then did a poo, A wet loose poo!

The inspectors, with their backs turned, were oblivious to what was happening, concentrating on the task in hand. Molly stooped and picked up the puppy whilst Iris put herself in front of the faecal matter hoping the inspectors would not turn around at that moment. Molly left the room, returning and joining Iris having secured the puppy in the lounge. They stood side by side in front of the mess which was beginning by now to let off an odour. Not daring to look at each other in case they were to start laughing.

"Everything seems to be in order" said Susan until her nose started to twitch and an unpleasant smell began to fill her nostrils. "I will of course send you our assessment when I have completed it. Meantime, well done and keep up the excellent work."

"Thank you" said Molly as both inspectors started to walk towards the door, sniffing into the air as if trying to work out where the foul odour was coming from.

"Sometimes when a breeze is blowing, we get the smell of chickens wafting up from the bottom of the garden" Iris said quickly, alerting their eyes to the open window. It was the only excuse she could come up with and there was little to no breeze to speak of.

"If you are finished perhaps, you would both like a cup of tea" said Molly, ushering the pair out of the office back into her kitchen.

"Thank you but no, we have a busy schedule to get through today." This time it was Susan who answered for them both.

Iris quickly closed the adjoining door between the office and kitchen as the inspectors made ready to leave.

Sounds of yapping intermingled with whining sounds as well as the scratching at the door echoed from the lounge area, becoming louder as the ensemble moved towards the hallway. Molly was getting very anxious and felt uncomfortably hot.

"Well done, Molly, as I said your certificates should arrive in the post once we have processed all the information."

"That's wonderful thank you" says Molly relieved. This time both inspectors extended a handshake.

"By the way I have just remembered where I have seen you before" says Susan Jameson causing Molly to have a hot flush and rendering her cheeks to blush.

"Yes, it was the Palomino hotel if I am not mistaken. I understood from the waiter you were there celebrating your birthday. I would like to say I hope you enjoyed it but as I recall you were VERY much enjoying it" she added with an emphasis on the word very.

"Yes, it was a lovely birthday present and I'm sorry if we were a bit silly. Champagne and the heat you know!" said Molly, wishing the ground would open and swallow her.

Molly opened the door.

"No need to apologise. I did a similar thing once in my YOUTH" she said smiling. This time the emphasis being on the word youth.

"I would just like to make one suggestion though if you don't mind" said Miles Faulkner as they were about to leave. "I noticed you have an exceptionally large garden. You should think about moving the chicken coup. If not, you could try banning the dog from the food preparation areas. Goodbye."

Nothing Ventured, Nothing Gained

Chapter 1

According to the meteorology calendar summer had been over since September and for Molly this could not have come to soon, that is if it had not been for the unexpected late extended summer.

In her youth Molly had lived for the warmth of the summer months. As students and with little money save what they had earnt from casual labour she and Simon had backpacked their way across the continents. Sometimes staying in hostels and sometimes sleeping under the moonlit skies gazing at the stars. Occasionally they had met up with similar like-minded students and had been invited to stay with them. Being young and in love, nothing worried them. They lounged on the hot sandy beaches and had swum naked in the warm seas.

It was years later that the intrepid and fearless couple had understood the heartache their parents must have felt when their own daughter had chosen to do similar.

Molly and Simon had settled into married life with a mortgage and all the rest of the bills that came with owning their own home. That was when they had to make cutbacks. When Laura had come along, they still managed a two-week break by saving throughout the year and would spend the time somewhere in Europe. All these memories felt so long ago now.

This summer had seemed never-ending. One of the hottest on record and Molly had flushed her way through it. Sweating night after night disturbing her sleep continued to take its toll. Molly would sometimes wake up feeling agitated and moody. Worst of all she knew she was beginning to get a bit forgetful but had been afraid to admit to this.

Unbeknown to Molly, Simon had also become concerned about this but decided to keep it to himself. He was extremely aware of how tetchy Molly had become. He was just riding the time when hopefully she would come out the other side of her menopause and he would have his fun-loving wife back.

October's orders had come in. For the first half of the month there had been no new customers. The regular supplies to coffee shops were all Molly and Iris had to bake for. The financial side of the business was going well, showing a healthy profit. They looked forward to an easy couple of weeks.

"Perhaps we should think about having a couple of days off Iris" suggested Molly as she was taking the last trays from the oven that morning.

"Sounds good to me Mol. I wouldn't mind spending some time with the grandkids. Haven't seen them since the summer hols" says Iris.

The telephone rang and Molly wiping her wet hands on a tea towel went to answer it. Iris only hearing one side of the conversation.

"Yes, I'm sure we can do that for you. Let me just check with my partner. You did say fifty, didn't you?" says Molly, turning to face Iris who smiled and nodded.

Molly confirmed the order, writing down the details in the diary as she went before signing off.

Twice more the phone rang in succession and twice more they accepted orders both and Molly wrote down the details.

"Don't worry Iris" says Molly, believing she saw disappointment in her friend's face. "Still time to have a few days break to catch up with the family. I can manage the prep work alone."

"If you are sure Mol that would be great. I will just take two days after the weekend and can be back on Wednesday" said Iris, to which Molly agreed.

It was not as if she had any grandchildren to visit like her friend had, Molly thought to herself, indulging in a little self-pity. She glanced at Iris who looked so contented as she worked her sugar magic.

It was only after Iris had finished for the day and left and Molly was about to turn off the lights that the phone rang again. Just for a moment her initial thought was "to hell with it! Let it ring." She could smell the aroma of the fresh coffee coming from her kitchen and guessed that Simon was home.

Her business head dictated she should however answer it. Another order was confirmed, and Molly looked for the diary. For some reason, the diary was not to hand, so she tore a piece of paper from a pad and wrote down the customer's details.

"I can phone Iris later" she thought. "I know she won't mind. Coffee first" and she turned off the light and closed the door behind her.

Simon held out a mug of coffee for her as she entered the kitchen. He thought she was looking tired. Vanda ran across the kitchen to greet her, jumping at her legs and yapping for attention. Molly bent down to make a fuss of the little puppy. The pet had become part of their family and had filled a small hole in Molly's heart.

"That's great!" says Simon jokingly. "When he gets your attention before me." Molly smiled.

That evening Molly phoned Iris with the information of this latest order, reassuring her once again that she would manage all the preparation. Iris was pleased.

"I've got some fun ideas for Halloween cake toppers" Iris told her. "I will sketch them down and let you see them. Rob says he can easily make the moulds."

"That sounds wonderful Iris. I look forward to seeing them but enjoy your break first. You truly deserve some time off. Both of you." Molly emphasized both and meaning it: "Give my love to the family and I will see you next week."

Chapter 2

The following week Molly and Iris, over a cup of coffee, discussed the forthcoming Halloween baking.

"I hope I haven't overstretched us, and we can manage three large orders like these" says Molly, excitedly reading out the details from her diary.

"Don't you mean four?" says Iris.

Molly appeared confused and looked at the diary again.

"No, just three" she replies, going through the pages a second time.

"My mistake!" says Iris. "Must have heard you wrong."

A thought process was now taking part in Molly's head and then the penny dropped.

"Oh, you silly arse!" she says aloud. "I am such a numbskull! I remember now. I couldn't find my diary, so I jotted an order on a piece of paper. I meant to write it in but must have forgotten."

Molly felt embarrassed. This was not the first time she had confessed to a lapse of forgetfulness. She was concerned that it could have impacted on their workload and ultimately the business.

"Don't worry Mol. I do it all the time" says Iris reassuringly, seeing Molly was looking worried. "And anyway, I think the order was for more cupcakes so that's easy." Molly continued to appear worried.

"We could always ask Pru to help us" says Iris grinning. She hoped that would make Molly smile. And it did.

"We would need to take out a hefty insurance in case we poisoned anyone." And they both laughed, and Molly began to relax.

"Seriously Iris I know I have said it before, but I don't know what I would do without you."

"We are a team and best friends and that's all that matters" Iris reminds her. "And besides I have never been so happy doing what we are doing."

With fresh coffee and left-over cake, they moved into Molly's lounge. Vanda following them.

Iris had brought her folder with her to show Molly the designs she had been working on for Halloween.

"I got Rob to practise with me using playdough last night and he wasn't half bad" Iris told Molly. "He managed to make some quite impressive spiders" she said, "even with his big hands."

"Perhaps I should consider employing him" Molly said jokingly.

As usual Iris came up trumps. Her designs were of a high degree of creativity. She had sketched out her ideas, made templates and worked out how she could apply them to fondant sugar icing and marzipan. Molly suggested the cake mixes should be naturally coloured to complement the various toppings.

The following day and for the next few days both Molly and Iris worked on the innovative ideas, applying them to their baking. They cut out and sculpted the marzipan and fondant sugar till they had made an assortment of spiders and webs, ghosts, and ghouls as well as witches on broomsticks. They even took the smaller pieces of icing and delicately worked them into golden sparkling moons and stars.

"All your ideas are utterly amazing Iris, but I think this time you have really surpassed yourself. I just cannot thank you enough" Molly said, hugging her friend.

"Thank you Mol, it's teamwork and I think we make a great team" she replied. And she meant it.

All four customers were pleased with their orders. The local paper displayed photos of the village children's Halloween party. Molly's Cupcakes got a mention too.

The incident over the forgotten order weighed heavily on Molly's mind and she could not put it behind her.

"Time for some changes!" she thought.

Chapter 3

It was Wednesday the following week when Molly had an appointment with her hairdresser. Without any deliberation, she had decided to make a radical change to what she had always referred to as her boring hair style.

Over the past few months, she had noticed that her hair had become drier and was turning even more grey. At first it had just been her roots. With the help of Simon, she could deal with this. He had become quite a dab hand with a box of hair dye that Molly would occasionally bring home from the chemist. Molly thought the time had now come when she wanted something completely different and decided to seek expert advice.

She had watched a TV programme called (Feel better Look better) just a few days previously where the host presenter had introduced three ordinary women from the public. All chosen because they were going through the menopause. Molly thought to herself ironically that they may have also been chosen because they looked drab. She hoped she did not look as bad as she thought they did. At least not yet.

The chosen three openly discussed their symptoms and anxieties. A panel of two women and two men, experts in their chosen fields of medicine, psychology, and beauty, listened before asking them questions.

Afterwards the three women had the opportunity to ask questions of the panel of experts. Molly did not believe that between them they could have had much in the way of personal experience at all. Two presenters being men and one woman looking as if she should still be at school. She thought the only one who could know anything would be the psychologist who looked at least to be somewhere in her forties.

Molly had been at home alone that evening. With a glass of wine in one hand and the TV controls in the other she flicked through the channels dismissing most of the discussion and banter that the programme had to offer because she believed that no one could tell her anything she did not already know. Flicking it back just in time to see the final part when all three women had returned to the set dressed in a new set of clothes, wearing makeup, and exhibiting new hairstyles. Then she did show a little more interest. They all looked so different and more importantly younger in appearance. Molly knew exactly what she was going to do. And she decided, she would not tell anyone. Not even Simon.

Chapter 4

As was the usual, Simon got out of bed first. He had been woken by the yapping sounds coming from the kitchen downstairs. This had become a daily ritual now and had left the alarm clock redundant. A quick visit to the bathroom to relieve himself before dressing in his two-piece tracksuit and rushing downstairs. He knew if he did not get to the dog quickly there would be even more scratches added to the almost bare wood of the painted kitchen door. As well as this there would be the usual puddle or two for him to clean up.

"I'm coming Vanda" he called as he hastily went down the stairs only to trip on one of Vanda's toys that had been left on one of the stairs. He fell down the last three steps awkwardly onto the wooden floor, oh! bollocks he shouted, and letting out an almighty yell.

Molly was now fully awake.

"What's happened" she shouted, reaching for her wrap.

By this time Vanda started to whimper loudly and the scratching at the door was becoming excessive.

"I think I've broken my arm" says Simon wincing and then moaning loudly as if trying to compete with the sounds coming from behind the kitchen door.

Molly got to him quickly.

"I don't think it's broken," said Molly as she examined it more closely and became aware that Simon was moving it easily. She helped him to his feet before rescuing the puppy from the kitchen. Vanda bounded past her in search of his alpha male, jumping and licking him all over.

"It's alright boy, daddy's ok" he told him. Gently pushing him down he encouraged Vanda to follow him back to the kitchen.

Molly, being first to notice the multiple puddles and the poo on the floor, collected the bucket from the utility containing a disinfectant solution. Donning an oversize pair of pink rubber gloves and pulling out a wad of disposable wipes she proceeded to clean up the mess.

"I think I'm ok" says Simon rubbing his arm and then circling it in the air. "Sorry Mol didn't expect you to have to deal with the mess" he added when he saw her on her hands and knees. "I did try and get to him quickly."

"I want to say not quick enough but inappropriate under the circumstances" she said with a straight face and then grinning behind his back, "Are you sure you're, ok?"

"I'm fine now thanks" he said, still rubbing his elbow. "I bet I will have a large bruise later to show for it though. I had better get this one out before he makes another mess. No time to make the coffee!" he says over his shoulder as he attaches the dog's lead.

Simon found himself dragged out of the back door and almost tripped over the step. He managed to stabilise himself and avoided falling flat on his face. Molly smiled.

Molly had already informed Simon of her plans to be up early that morning to go shopping. She had things to organise before herself and Iris would be going away on Friday and staying overnight. Being a working day for Simon, she did not want to leave Vanda for more than a few hours on his own.

Two cups of coffee later, with Molly's second one being consumed on the go in between her showering and dressing, Molly was ready and set off into town.

Katie, her hairdresser, who had cut Molly's hair for the last few years, had been surprised by her adamant request to cut, colour and restyle her client's hair. She had always thought that she would have liked to do something a bit more exciting than the usual short bob that Molly had insisted on but did have concern's that she might be taking it to the extreme. That is until she saw what Molly had wanted her to do.

Molly took out the magazine cutting and unfolded the piece of paper to show her.

"What do you think Katie" Molly asks. "Too young looking for me?

"Not at all Molly" Katie said truthfully. "I think it would work very well and if you don't like it, we can always change it."

The wash, cut and highlights took longer than her usual visit to the hairdressers. Molly settled back in the chair and relaxed, enjoying the pampering. She especially enjoyed the cup of coffee that Katie's assistant made for her and which she drank whilst reading a magazine and sitting under the hair dryer. With the heat from the dryer and her caffeine hit came the inevitable hot flush. Katie saw how uncomfortably red and hot Molly was becoming. She quickly brought her out from underneath the dryer and offered her a glass of chilled water from the cooler.

"Don't worry Molly" says Katie, concerned that Molly was feeling embarrassed. "This happens a lot."

Taking deep breaths as well as drinking the water helped to desensitise Molly's sense and the drying was able to continue.

Molly watched in the mirror as Katie worked the comb through her hair creating the final look. Katie in her turn talked Molly through how to do the same after washing her hair at home.

"Well, what do you think" asked Katie, pleased with her creativity and eagerly hoping for a positive reply.

"I like it very much; it will take a bit of getting used to."

"It takes years off you" says Katie who had really meant it, which was not always the case with one or two of her other clients.

Molly walked through the town with a spring in her step stopping occasionally to look at her reflection in a window while pretending to browse the window display. Shopping completed she drove home to wait for her husband's response which she knew would have to wait till he had returned from work.

Vanda had been a little unsure of his owner at first until he sniffed around her and then received the usual pat on her head.

"Wow! Where is my Mol?" Simon teased when he first glimpsed his wife. "I like it!" he says as she twirled herself, smiling in front of him.

"Do you still fancy me?" Molly asked teasingly.

"You bet I do! Shall we go upstairs now so I can prove it?"

"Don't think so, you might spoil my new hairdo."

"You know something Mol! I am so glad you had red streaks and not purple ones" mocked Simon, causing Molly to laugh.

"Perhaps next time eh!"

"Before I forget I took a message for you just as I was about to leave this morning. I wrote it down and put it on your desk. It was just a small order for twenty cupcakes with a football theme for a Mrs Randall's son's birthday, and I knew you were not overly busy this month, so I said yes and before you say anything I did check your diary" informed Simon.

"Thanks Si, I'm sure that's ok."

Molly was in a good mood today and nothing she thought would change that. After quickly checking the note Molly was a little disappointed when she realised the order had been for thirty cup-cakes instead of the twenty that Simon had said and for a birthday party on Sunday the ninth.

Molly and Iris did not plan to be back until late on the Saturday as they had decided to go shopping after the event and have a meal in London. Following a discussion with Iris they had agreed that they would have enough time to shop and be back to bake the cakes in the evening.

"I have some fondant sugar ready, enough to make pairs of boots and I will get Rob to help make some tiny footballs this evening" said Iris "Shouldn't take me long as I have made some before."

Molly insisted on helping and Iris agreed. "Then we will both have plenty of time to pack" she said.

Friday morning after she had showered, Molly took a comb and proceeded to style her hair the way Katie had shown her. Choosing a more flamboyant outfit for the occasion, matching it with a piece of costume jewellery and a suitable pair of shoes that she thought would go with her ensemble, she stood in front of the full-length mirror admiring herself.

She checked her lightly made-up face and sprayed herself with her favourite perfume. A quick glance in the mirror and she was ready. "Not bad for a fifty-year-old!" she said, making a final twirl.

"Mol, you look amazing. I feel a bit underdressed and dowdy next to you" said Iris, admiring her friend's new hairstyle and what she had been wearing. "Don't suppose I've got time to change my outfit" Iris asked checking the time on her watch.

"Iris, you look great as you always do." Molly meant every word. To her mind Iris had always dressed well. Molly thought she had a quirky sort of knack when it came to putting colours and styles together. "So, no you haven't got time to change, and you really don't need to" Molly insisted, helping Iris with her large suitcase into the back of her van.

"How many changes of clothes do you have in there? We are only away overnight" Molly teased.

"I know but I do like to be prepared for any eventuality."

They set off in Rosie to the cake decorating convention that they had booked tickets for. Because the fair was being held in a London hotel, they had booked a room to stay in the same. They had both been looking forward to the event and hoped that they would come back with some innovative ideas for the expanding Molly's cupcake business.

Chapter 5

Simon returned home earlier than was usual. He had no lectures that afternoon and did not fancy leaving Vanda on his own for too long. He was greeted by a dog that had forgotten that he had been walked that morning and now that his master had returned, he was ready to go out again.

"Have to be a quick one" he said making the usual fuss of petting the dog. "I've still got work to do you know." Thirty minutes later and Vanda settled down in his bed. Simon had only just opened his laptop when Vanda appeared at his side. He began to pester him by placing his front paws on his lap. With his tail wagging he started to yap at him for attention. No matter how hard he tried he would not give in.

"Ok! You win" he said leading the puppy into the garden with his favourite ball. "Only for a few minutes, I have a lot of work to get done."

For ten minutes he threw the ball and ran around the garden as if chasing him. Vanda had not learnt the art of bringing the ball back yet. In fact, he had not learnt anything yet except to sit when commanded.

"Puppy training classes are definitely something we must sort out" he told the dog as no matter how hard he tried he could not make him leave the ball. "Enough is enough" he said, "I really must get on."

The puppy followed his master back inside the house and proceeded to wee on the kitchen floor.

"You bad boy" he shouted. "Especially when you were just outside" he told him wagging his finger before he fetched the bucket of disinfectant from the cupboard. Vanda was beginning to identify the tone in his owners' voices and had not liked it when his master had raised his voice. He sulked out of the kitchen leaving Simon to clean up the mess.

Simon made himself a cup of instant coffee before returning to his study. He was just in time to witness Vanda pulling papers from his desk and once again shouted at him to leave. This time he had not been perturbed by his master's anger and continued shaking his head tearing at the papers with his teeth. Simon had to chase him around the room to retrieve them.

"You bad boy" he says in a harsh voice. "To the kitchen with you."

Simon put the puppy into its bed and told him sternly to stay. Vanda, who was now tired, curled up and settled down to sleep and Simon returned to his study to work. He had only just started to read the first document flagged up in his inbox when the phone rang, and he swore at the intrusion.

"Hello, can I speak with Molly please" came the voice on the other end of the phone.

"Sorry she isn't here; can I take a message?"

"Oh, you must be her husband, we spoke on the phone recently. I was just wondering if I could collect the cakes at five o'clock for my son's party."

Simon was dumbstruck.

"Hello, can you hear me?" came the voice on the other end of the phone.

"Sorry, yes I, I, can hear you" replied Simon, stammering. "Let me just check the order" he continued to say knowing full well that no cakes had been baked for that day. He deliberately rattled papers on his desk to make believe he had been checking the order. Simon needed to think, and quickly at that.

"Oh yes of course, here it is. Mrs Randall, isn't it? And yes, they will be ready for five o'clock" he said.

"Phew" came the caller on the other end of the phone. "You had me worried there for a minute, but I knew Molly would not let me down. I will see you at five."

"They will be ready for you. See you then Mrs Randall" he said quickly before replacing the phone.

Simon sat at his desk and panic set in. Never had he been in a situation like this. He clenched both fists trying to think of a solution. This was something he did when looking for a way out. He knew Molly would be angry at his cock-up.

"How on earth had I managed to get the date so wrong" he thought to himself. He scoured the untidy papers on his desk looking for the order he had scribbled down and found it. He had written down that the birthday boy would be eight years old on the ninth when in fact he should have written nine years on the eighth. "Dam and blast, what the hell am I going to do" he spoke aloud to himself.

With only a few hours before Mrs Randall was due to collect her order, he knew he had to find a solution. He needed someone who could help him and could only think of one mate.

"Simple!" says Rob from his office phone. "I haven't got a lot on, so can be with you shortly. You my friend are going to be Molly, and I will be Iris. I'm sure we can bake a few simple cupcakes; it cannot be that difficult."

Simon did not know what to say. The idea that the two of them could pass themselves off as bakers was incomprehensible. Neither of them had ever baked a cake in their lives.

Vanda followed his master through into the kitchen and then into Molly's office.

"Oh no you don't" says Simon picking him up and placing him firmly in his bed. "You will have to stay there; this is an emergency!"

Rob did not need an excuse to leave the mountain of paperwork on his desk. The pile of papers, which had increased two-fold was boring filing. He knew he could leave it until Janie got back from her holiday. She had managed to get everything up to date before she left.

"The invoices are complete, and the wages are sorted, and the filing can wait till I get back" she had told him as she hurried to get out of the office. It was easy to lose track of time, and she had only meant to work a couple of hours that morning.

"Thanks Janie, now off you go and enjoy your holiday" Rob had told her.

Janie only worked for Rob two days a week. She was supposed to be retired but was getting bored after the first six months at home on her own. She had been pleased when Rob offered her a part time job. Being a mature woman, she was not sure she would be in the running for the position. Rob on the other hand had thought Janie highly suitable. A very skilled and conscientious worker and easy to get on with. She also made a particularly good cup of tea.

By the time he got to Simon's house it was almost twelve noon. He knocked on the door and let himself in as was usually the case. Rob was greeted by a very noisy puppy who yapped and jumped up against his leg seeking attention. Vanda had gotten use to Rob and Iris as they were frequent visitors to the house.

"Hello Vanda, where's your master then" he said gently pushing him down and making a fuss of the dog.

"In here" shouted Simon from Molly's office. He had been looking through recipe books trying to find a suitable one to use.

"Thanks for coming over, Rob, I really have made a balls up! of this one" says Simon as he went on to explain to his friend how he had messed up the order. "I did think about giving Pru a ring, but I don't think Mol would have approved, best to keep this one between ourselves."

"No worries" says Rob. "I reckon this could be fun" he joked to his friend seeing the worried look on Simon's face.

"First things first, I better try and get some of this engine oil off my hands, Iris is always telling me to wash them before cooking" he said.

Rob rolled up his sleeves as he made his way to the sink. He turned on the tap and let the hot water flow over his dirty hands. He applied a generous amount of the antibacterial soap from the dispenser and began to wash his hands. He soon realised that no amount of rubbing and scrubbing was going to remove all the grease from his hands. "That will just have to do" he exclaimed after examining them and went to dry them on the towel. "Whoops!" he says aloud when he sees just how much black stain he had left on the towel.

"I think Mol keeps some plastic gloves somewhere" says Simon when he saw that Rob's hands were not looking much cleaner. He pulled open drawers and checked in the cupboards but could not find any.

"Don't worry Si, time isn't on our side and a little bit of grease won't hurt anyone" says Rob, raising his hands as if to admire them.

Together they took out the various ingredients from the cupboards that they thought they might need. Simon found a recipe that he thought would be suitable and easy to follow. They began to measure out massive quantities of butter, sugar, and flour into two mixing bowls. There was no time to mix anything by hand, so Rob chose two electric hand whisks. They turned the whisks on high power and proceeded to combine the ingredients expelling clouds of flour into the air. Both turned off their machines.

"Oh, dear I think we need to add eggs and milk!" Rob read out. "Any idea where I can find them?"

"Oh blast! I was supposed to collect them from the chickens this morning, but I forgot" says Simon.

"No probs mate" says Rob, "I can do that."

"And I will get some milk."

Simon reread the recipe to make sure he had added everything except the eggs and milk. Written at the bottom of the recipe was a list of flavours that could also be added to the mixture, and he chose a bottle of vanilla. He was beginning to feel a bit smug. "Not as difficult as she makes out" he thought to himself.

He could see Rob from the window making his way back up the garden path. He had forgotten to take a container and was carrying a load of eggs in both hands. Rob pleased with himself, lifted his hands higher to show Simon the produce he had collected. He was walking fast and not looking where he was treading when he missed his footing, tripping on a loose paving slab he fell to the ground. Simon having seen his friend fall rushed to his aid.

"It's ok I'm alright" says Rob getting to his feet and brushing himself down. "Nothing broken" he said.

"You think so" says Simon noticing the eggs that lay smashed on the ground.

"Oh bugger! And I got all of them. How quickly do chickens lay their eggs?" Rob asked, unsuccessfully trying to make a joke.

"Guess I will have to give Pru a ring after all" says Simon.

"No, you will not, it's ok because I am sure Iris will have eggs at home. You get the cake papers ready for the mix and I will pop and get them."

Again, Simon read the recipe, and it was just as well as he realised that he needed to warm the oven. He turned on the oven, carefully setting the suggested temperature. Having already added a spoonful of vanilla he bravely decided to add a little essence of lemon. Rob returned with some more eggs and this time they were in boxes. Together they cracked the number of eggs that they had already calculated to be the right number.

"Here goes" says Simon turning on the mixer to full speed, which sent plumes of white flour again into the air. Rob suggested he reduced the speed to a less vigorous one like he was doing. They watched the bowls as the ingredients began to blend. Both men were feeling incredibly pleased with themselves. Minutes ticked by, and the mixture was what they thought to be ready.

Both men taking their index finger dipped them into the mixture.

"Well here goes" says Rob as they both sucked off the creamy mixture.

"That's not at all bad" says Rob and Simon agreed.

They found the next step a little trickier. Nowhere in the recipe did it say just how much or how little mixture, they should put into the baking papers or how to do it. They decided to use teaspoons and counted out four to each paper case. With a little left over they filled the ones that looked as if they had a little less than others. Simon and Rob took the filled trays and transferred them into the hot oven.

"One thing I remember Iris telling me was that you should never be tempted to open the oven door until the cooking time is completed" says Rob to Simon.

"Well, there must be a reason for it, but I can't imagine what that might be" Simon mocked teasingly, inwardly admiring his friend's knowledge of baking. He thought that he too might have picked up a few things relating to the art of baking from Molly, but he had not- at least he couldn't think of anything at that moment.

While the cakes were baking the men set to, making butter icing. Simon read out the instructions.

"I think we'd better make two bowls of the stuff" suggested Rob. "There is a lot of cakes to cover."

Taking a large bowl each and a spoon, they measured out the ingredients according to the recipe. Tossing the icing sugar into the bowls created more clouds of dust which made them laugh and make pretend they needed to cough.

"I can taste the sugar" said Simon who then, with a wide mouth, tried to catch more dust. As is always the case when one does something so silly the other must copy. Deliberately they both lifted their sugar sifts higher and began to shake them. The motion creating even more dust. Making fishlike sounds with their mouths they continued to try and catch the sweet clouds of sugar. After some more mixing the dust settled and they both concentrated on creaming the mixture.

"Do you think we should add a spoon of lemon flavour like I put in the cake mix? asked Simon.

"Yep, and better put some of this yellow colouring in as well" agreed Rob.

Again, both tasted the finished mixture before deciding to add a little more lemon.

It was just as they finished preparing the topping mixture that the oven alarm rang signalling that the cooking time was up. Eagerly they opened the door to see whether the cakes were cooked. Not only were they cooked, but they were well and truly risen and filled the paper cases. Simon thought they looked a lot bigger than the ones Molly made. They were both pleased with the result.

"This cake making is a lot easier than Mol makes out," says Simon.

"Don't know what all the fuss is about" agreed Rob.

"I've just remembered something I did learn from Mol and that is to let the cakes cool before decorating them," said Simon.

Rob already knew this to be the case, and he agreed. It made sense to him. He thought anyone would know that.

"Time for a cup of tea Rob?"

"You put the kettle on while I pop home and fetch the football boots and balls that Iris made for decorations."

"OK I had better check on the dog too. He has been noticeably quiet!"

Simon found Vanda still in his bed. As he approached him the animal started wagging his tail but never attempted to leave his bed. "Sorry mate did not mean to get so cross, but I did have a panic situation on my hands. Thanks to Uncle Rob it is all sorted now. I will make it up to you later I promise."

Rob returned with a tray full of tiny pairs of football boots and balls that the customer had ordered and placed them on the table.

"Your Iris is very talented" said Simon eyeing the collection.

"I'll have you know I made some of these" boasted Rob. "Quite easy when you get the hang of it."

"Perhaps we should start our own cupcake business" Simon jests as he pours them both a mug of tea.

It took several attempts for Simon and Rob, as they practised icing one of the cakes before deciding that Rob was the better at it. With less than forty minutes before the cakes were due to be collected by Mrs Randall there was no time to lose. So, Rob iced while Simon added a small pair of boots, and a football decoration made from fondant icing to each cupcake. All that remained to do was the packaging. The task completed and only just in time.

Mrs Randall arrived a little before five o'clock eager to collect her order. She was greeted at the door by the two men, both with white powder on their faces.

"Looks like you two have been helping Molly today" she said teasingly as she lifted the lid off one of the boxes.

Peeping inside she was delighted with its contents.

"I must thank Molly and Iris before I go" said Mrs Randall, pushing her way through the hall towards the kitchen. "I know where it is" she says referring to Molly's office.

"Neither of them is in there. They had to pop out for something. Not sure when they will get back," lied Simon, trying to block her way.

"Oh, that is a shame. I will not have time to phone later but tell her I will call her tomorrow. You must be so proud of them" she says to both men as she turned to leave, making her way to her car. Simon and Rob helped to carry the boxes and placed them safely on the back seat as requested.

"Phew!" they both said simultaneously. "That was a narrow escape. Put it their mate" said Simon raising a hand to do a high five.

"I think we both deserve a drink after that."

"I think more than one might be in order" exclaimed Rob. "Why don't we go over to mine; I was going to invite you over for dinner anyway with the girls away."

"Sounds great! Ok if I bring Vanda along?"

"Of course you can. He is one of the family now" Rob replied bending down to make a fuss of the dog who was trying to gain his attention.

"How does omelettes sound for supper? I make a mean omelette, even if I say so myself" suggests Rob.

"Don't you need eggs for that?" teased Simon.

"Oh yes I forgot we have used them all" replied Rob. The raucous sound of laughter caused Vanda to back away with his tail between his legs.

"It's ok boy" says Simon, picking the puppy up. "Didn't mean to scare you."

"When I get back, I will order a pizza instead. Think we might need to clean ourselves up a bit first though." suggested Rob.

"Good idea. See you in ten and I will bring bottles of beer. It is the least I can do."

Chapter 6

The following day Molly and Iris returned from their trip. They had been expecting to bake cakes that evening for Mrs Randall. Neither of them had felt much like baking cakes. After a packed two days the pair were tired so when Simon explained that they did not have to bake it came as quite a relief.

Initially Molly had been angry with Simon for mixing up the dates, but her feelings quickly changed to one of utter amazement and pride when he told her how they had managed to fulfil the order successfully and how Mrs Randall was none the wiser.

Molly and Iris went into the office. The men had used far more equipment than they themselves would have used. The units in Molly's office were a mess with dirty bowls and utensils as well as empty packets and boxes. Sticky cake mixture and icing was stuck fast to all surfaces. The floor was a mess, made worse by dirty paw prints.

"This is why I don't like men in my kitchen" said Molly and Iris agreed. For a few moments they just stood staring at the mess. Then looking at each other both shrugged their shoulders and started to giggle.

"Coffee first!" says Molly smiling, linking her arm through her friend's.

The Bonfire Night Massacre.

Chapter 1

With bonfire night just two days away it meant that both she and Iris would have two exceptionally busy, long days. As usual Molly and Iris had prepared well in advance. Preparation during these short periods between festivals was invaluable.

Iris once again producing innovative ideas suitable for the occasion.

There were just three orders for independent bakeries and two private parties. With Iris's usual creative ideas, they had both painted fireworks onto white and chocolate discs. These were to be the toppings for the cupcakes. Using chocolate shavings, they made tiny bonfires with red tops giving the appearance of burning.

Molly had been asked to design and make a large chocolate bonfire-shaped cake for a surprise fiftieth birthday celebration. She started by baking two exceptionally large chocolate cakes. Having creamed them together she then set about sculpting the desired shape representing a bonfire. The next phase was to cover the shape in chocolate fondant icing ready for Iris's artistic skills.

"Wow! Molly, you managed to shape this one perfectly," said Iris. "I hope I can do it justice."

"I have every confidence in you Iris. I am in no doubt that it will be perfect."

Molly watched on as Iris worked her pens.

Firstly, choosing red, orange, and yellow as the main colours, Iris began to work her artistic flair. Then by adding gold and silver she created the bright sparks and embers of a bonfire. It truly looked as if the cake was burning. The perfecting touch was to add small sparklers which could be lit just before the cake was cut.

"This is definitely one for the album" said Simon, walking in on them as they had just completed the final additions, gloating over what he called a true masterpiece.

Every year on a suitable day around the 5th of November the village came together to celebrate Guy Fawkes or bonfire night. The local scout group would oversee collecting burning material and building the fire on the village green. The making and burning of an effigy of Fawkes himself no longer took place. At least not in their village. It had been the teachers from the local schools and supported by the churches who had made the decision to stop what they believed to be an unnecessary barbaric influence for the village children.

The focus was on the firework display. This was organised and paid for by the rotary club. As well as the firework display there would be food stalls selling hotdogs and burgers as well as toffee apples and similar treats. Farmer Brown always provided a cider tent where adults could buy an alcoholic beverage. His speciality on this occasion being mulled cider with honey which always tasted delicious. Once again it was Oli with his son Andy who would provide the musical entertainment.

Last year the scouts had asked Molly if she would like to donate some of her baking specials. Molly, after giving it some thought, had suggested she could bake apple cakes.

"Molly that would be great. I am sure dad can supply you with apples from the farm. It has been a bumper crop this year" Jack had told her.

"Do you think that's due to the wassail?" Molly teased him as she recalled the merriments of that evening back in January.

"The best one ever! It took a while for dad to come round to the idea but even he enjoyed it, and he says we must make it a regular event," said Jack.

Just like the previous year, farmer Brown delivered buckets full of apples to Molly's house in plenty of time.

Molly remembered how quickly they had sold out that previous year so was determined that this should not happen again. Unlike last year when Molly had made the cakes by herself, this year, she was concerned that baking even more cakes would be a task too great for her alone. She need not have worried. It was Iris who having remembered buying a whole cake, brought up the subject of baking and offered her help.

"But Iris" said Molly, "I make the cakes for free so the scouts can make some money."

"I know but I would still like to help you. I appreciate it benefits the community too."

"Thanks Iris. I could do with borrowing any cake tins you might think suitable as well."

"How's about us asking Pru to help" suggests Iris. "She's always saying how she wants to be more involved in the village community."

"Do you think I should?" Iris nods. "Ok let me give her call" says Molly.

Pru was EVER so keen.

"I have never made apple cakes before, and I would love to learn. Shall I bring Michael along as well if Simon and Rob are helping?" says Pru.

Everyone agreed that the more hands they had, would make the task easier.

Chapter 2

Early in the morning of the day before the bonfire and on a cold damp and windy November day Molly, Iris and Pru, with their partners, came together in Molly's office to make large apple cakes.

When Simon had seen the buckets of apples that covered the doorstep, he too was grateful for the troupes. The three men worked alongside each other at the sinks. They started with two of them peeling while one diced. As the peeled apple began to pile up, they switched to one peeling while two of them sliced and diced.

"When the bowl is full Mike" says Simon, "just squeeze a little lemon juice over them that stops them going to brown."

"Becoming quite a baker now aren't we" teased Rob.

Rob threw a piece of apple peel at him which landed on the floor and Iris saw it.

"Now you boys none of that" says Iris with a straight face.

"Consider yourself told off mate" whispered Simon. All three men began to chuckle.

Across the room both Molly and her helpers were rubbing the butter into the flour. They were already on their second and third bowls. On the side were bowls of sugar already weighed out and smaller bowls of a mixture of spices. Pru was keen to know the type and ratio of spices that Molly used.

"I have always kept it to myself, but I will of course write it down for you both," said Molly.

"Now If you two don't mind starting to grease the tins I will go and get the eggs" suggests Molly.

There was a lot of laughter coming from the sink where the men were working. Molly glanced at them as she was leaving the room and was just in time to see Mike and Rob attempting to see which of them could peel an apple the fastest leaving the peel in one piece. Molly smiled.

It was good to see the three men getting on so well, she thought to herself as she closed the door behind her.

Simon stopped slicing. He scoured the back of a drawer underneath the sink looking for a third peeler. Taking out an old-fashioned looking one which he did not recognise he proceeded to join in.

"I hope you aren't peeling too thickly" Iris says having noticed large curls of peelings that had missed the bowl and now lay on the ground.

"No worries" says Simon. "We've still got plenty of apples to peel."

"Yes, and we still have more cakes to bake" says Iris, concerned that it may have been Rob who had instigated the game.

"Damn and blast!" shouts Simon, so everyone turns to see what has happened.

"Only gone and sliced my hand" he says just as Molly returns with the eggs.

"You bloody fool. What have you done? Let me see" she says.

Molly quickly takes charge. Uncurling his fingers she quickly held his hand under cold running water. Iris fetches the first aid box. Blood has dripped into and all over the bowl of chopped apples in front of him.

Rob and Mike stopped their game as Pru scowled and they considered themselves reprimanded.

"Will need to throw the whole bowl full out now. Waste of time! waste of time!" she muttered.

"Don't think it looks to bad" says Molly, drying the wound on Simon's hand before closely examining it. "I knew I should have got rid of that old peeler. Only kept it for sentimental reasons. It belonged to my great granny."

"No more peeling for you Si" says Iris as she helps Molly to dress Simon's wound.

"And you have wasted a whole bowl of apples" added Pru again, this time looking directly towards Michael as if it were he who was the one to blame.

Rob and Mike finished off peeling the last of the apples while Simon, with his one hand, started picking up the fallen pieces.

With their backs turned on the women all three men started to chuckle again. Pulling faces and mimicking the fact that they had all been reprimanded. This time more quietly.

The chickens had been out of their pen as was always the case at this time of the day. Vanda being safely in his bed in the kitchen.

Molly commented to Iris and Pru how well her hens were still laying. She was proud to show off the basket of large eggs she had just collected.

Overall, it had been a fun morning in the office save of course for Si's accident. The men were keen to learn how to make the apple cakes and wanted to help with more than just preparing the fruit, so they looked on as the women completed the work, occasionally being allowed to whisk eggs, add ingredients and mix the contents. Albeit under the watchful eyes of the true bakers.

For Iris and Pru (Enjoy)

MOLLY'S (GRANDMOTHER'S)
APPLE CAKE RECIPE

8 oz. Self-Raising Flour

4 oz. Butter

4oz. Brown Sugar

2 Eggs

Molly's Spice

8oz. Cooking Apples Peeled and Chopped

4oz. Raisins soaked overnight in a spoon full of calvados –
    Optional and for adults only!

Just Enough Milk to Make the Mixture Sticky

METHOD

Rub Fat into Flour

Mix In Sugar, Spices and Chopped Apple

Add In the Well-Beaten Eggs

Slowly Add Milk to the right sticky consistency

Turn Into Greased and Lined 8in. Cake tin

Bake for 1 hour and 15 minutes!

At 180 degrees centigrade

Or 350 degrees Fahrenheit

Or Gas Mark 4

Sh! 1 teaspoon Cinnamon   (Tweak spices to suit palate)

Half teaspoon Nutmeg
Quarter teaspoon of Ginger and clove Powder

The cakes were baked in batches. In between the baking the six of them enjoyed more than one mug of coffee and warm slices of the first apple cake to come out of the oven. By mid-afternoon, the baking was completed, and the cakes were left to cool.

In previous years, the four had enjoyed a pub supper together before attending the firework display but this year would have to be different. This was Vanda's first firework experience, so Molly and Simon had decided to stay home for the first part of the evening with their dog, agreeing to meet up with their friends for food and mulled cider later.

Chapter 3

Molly drove Rosie to deliver the cakes in plenty of time. She had wanted to get back to take Vanda for a good walk with Simon. It was likely that they would be out late into the evening.

Molly need not have worried as Vanda did not react too badly to the echoing sounds of the fireworks as they started to go off. From their bedroom window she and Simon could still enjoy the display as the clear night skies lit up with white and coloured sparks of explosive patterns. Vanda barked and then whimpered just twice on hearing a dulled bang sound in the distance.

"It's alright boy" Simon said, bending down to reassure him.

Being a small village affair, the display of fireworks did not last long. Molly settled Vanda in his bed before they both went out to join their friends. The smell of gunpowder wafting up their nostrils as their walk took them closer to the village.

Molly was eager to try the mulled cider and went straight to the tent. Iris and Rob were already there.

"Where's Si?" asks Iris, getting off her stool to greet her friend. "Hope his hand is ok."

"He is fine. I did need to redress it again before we came out. I have left him going to get his first hotdog" Molly said smiling, knowing it would not be his last if last year was anything to go by.

This was one of the rare occasions when Molly allowed herself to drink cider, usually preferring to drink wine. Having drunk her first cupful she soon realised that it might have been better if she too had eaten something first. The warming honey-sweet cider tasted delicious and morish. The effects of the alcohol beginning to make her relax and tiddly.

By the time Simon joined them she was enjoying a second cup.

"I'm ready for a burger" says Molly, who remembered that she had missed supper.

They all agreed they were ready for something to eat and went in search of the burger stall.

"Don't remember having to queue for food like this last year" says Iris.

"I'm surprised you can remember much of last year after the hangover you had" teased Rob.

Simon having eaten two hotdogs still managed to eat a large burger with all the trimmings.

Molly was keen to see if the slices of apple cakes were selling. She left the others who were returning to the tent and went in search of the cake stall. A queue was forming there as well. Ray, the senior scout leader, saw her approach and went to greet her. Walking along by his side was his son Zac. Molly thought how good-looking Ray was. And how his son had inherited his father's genes. Man, and boy stepping out proudly and immaculately dressed in their scout uniforms.

She recognised Zac as one of the Pound- a-job-week scouts who came to her house with an offer of doing jobs for her earlier in the year. She had teased them about how it was once known as bob-a-job week. By the look on their faces, they had heard this too many times.

244 | MOLLY MUNDAY'S CUPCAKES

He and two others had worked hard with the jobs they had been allotted. She had given them five pounds each as well as large pieces of chocolate cake. They had been so polite and appreciative.

Ray put out his hand to greet her and his son followed suit.

"Thank you so much for your generosity, Molly" he says, taking her hand in a firm grip. The warmth of his hand sending a tingle down her spine.

Molly thinks to herself, "Grow up you silly old woman, you're old enough to be his mother."

"Yes, thank you again Mrs Molly," says Zac. "The apple cake is delicious, and I've already eaten two pieces."

"Not just me this year to thank. I had my own troops to help" she smiled, pointing out and beckoning Iris and Pru forward and looping her arms through theirs.

"Let me introduce you" she says.

"Don't forget us. We helped as well" says Rob as he and Mike came forward to join the group.

"They are selling very well, and as my son says they taste delicious" says Ray, shaking hands with the two men as well. "We've already eaten two pieces haven't we Zac."

"And we are going to get some to go with our cider" says Rob.

"Better hurry its selling fast" Ray smiles, and the men head off towards the table.

"We will let you know how much we have managed to raise" he told Molly. "And thank you again from all of us."

Back at the cider tent the music was in full swing. People were joining in singing the choruses while others were dancing on the spot as there was little room to move. The bright coloured lightbulbs around the tent illuminating the buzzing atmosphere. Rob squeezed his way through to the bar where he purchased four more large cups of cider. Many of their friends had gathered there including David and Sacha who had closed the pub for the evening so they could attend. It was difficult holding conversation because of the noise but everyone was having an enjoyable time.

Most of the children had now gone home due to the lateness of the evening. Some, it seemed, reluctantly as moans of unfairness could be overheard, while others were in tears.

The bonfire was still burning but much less ferociously. The older in the community gathered around it for warmth. Some of them were enjoying waving the last of the handheld sparklers into the air.

In the cider tent the merriment continued. It was difficult to manoeuvre oneself around as the tent became even more crowded as people left the fire to return inside.

Molly felt an arm across her shoulder. In that moment she was relieved to know that Simon was close by, protecting her from the crowd. She stroked his hand before turning and kissing it.

"Here you all are then" came the loud voice beside her.

Molly suddenly realised the arm and hand that she had kissed did not belong to Simon. Embarrassed, she quickly shook it off and turned to face the owner. For a moment, their eyes fixed. He smiled. She blushed and panicked.

"Sorry, Vicar! I thought you were my husband. How lovely to see you here! Are you enjoying yourself? Is Louise with you? I hope you enjoyed the firework display." Molly chatted on grateful for the poor lighting that hid her blushing face. She hoped the others in their party would think it was just the cider that caused her face to flush.

"Call me Tom tonight please Molly, we are still friends are we not?" he says with a broad smile and a wink of his eye. Molly could not be sure but thought she had felt his hand on her back before the incident.

"Where's Louise?" asks Iris having observed Molly's predicament.

"She is just getting us both some more cider" he replied to the group. "It is a very good cider isn't it," this time addressing his comment to a very embarrassed Molly.

Tom suddenly spotted someone in the crowd.

"Please excuse me. I have just seen someone I need to talk to. Enjoy the rest of your evening" he says to the group before steering his wife, who was holding two cups of cider, in the direction of someone else.

"Phew!" says Molly.

"He really has a thing for you" teased Iris, whispering in Molly's ear.

Jenny, who had been helping Jack at the bar, moved between people collecting empty cups. George called out last orders for cider. His licence to sell ending at 10 o'clock giving him an hour to clean up.

Molly and Iris did not enjoy their last cup of cider that had been thrust upon them. Neither had really wanted another one. Both knowing they had drunk far too much.

The musicians stopped playing coinciding with the last call to the bar.

Iris managed to catch Rob's eye indicating it was time for them to leave. Simon and Mike also joined the women.

Pru and Michael walked with them as they were all going in the same direction. The men walked in front chatting and joking together. The three ladies following closely behind. As on another occasion they were all at levels of intoxication.

"Do you know something? I think the vicar has a thing about your wife" Pru said loudly, directing this to Simon in front. "He seems ever so friendly."

"That is because she has known him since primary school. Haven't you Mol?" said Iris.

"We were at school together Pru. Such a long time ago I hardly remember him" says Molly trying to change the subject.

"He obviously remembers you. I saw him put his arm around you too" says Pru. Molly could feel her heart racing and just wanted Pru to drop the subject and for them to get home.

"Fire's burning, Fire's burning" Pru starts to sing, and Molly tries not to read anything into the words.

"Draw nearer, draw nearer" they all sing.

"Fire! Fire, Fire! Fire! they all join in as they continue the walk home.

Vanda was pleased to see his owners return. He had left them a small puddle on the floor. This time however he had managed to use the newspaper that had been laid out on the kitchen floor. Well at least the corner of it!

Simon invited everyone in for coffee to which they had all accepted. This was one occasion when Molly had wished he had not. He ushered them into the lounge before cleaning up after Vanda and then set to making the coffee.

Molly offered more apple cake with their coffees to which they all accepted.

"You make a great coffee Simon" remarked Pru sipping the steaming liquid from her mug. She was beginning to feel accepted and was enjoying this new friendship.

"Have you told Simon about the vicar putting his arm around you Molly?"

"What was that?" asked the three men simultaneously.

Molly explained what she thought had been Simon's arm had indeed been the vicars. She did not tell him how she had caressed and kissed his hand though.

Pru saw the funny side of this and joined in with the laughter.

Iris, observing Molly, thought her friend was looking a bit uncomfortable and quickly changed the subject.

They all concluded it had been a successful village bonfire night.

After their guests had gone, Simon took Vanda for his last walk.

Eager to get to bed Molly collected a tray on which to carry the plates and mugs and the remains of the apple cake into the kitchen. Despite drinking her coffee Molly still felt a little tipsy when she stood upright.

The crockery would have to wait until tomorrow to wash up, she thought to herself as she carried the full tray into the kitchen.

Failing to notice one of Vanda's toys that had been left on the floor she stepped on it, momentarily losing her balance. She had saved herself from falling over, but the tray went crashing to the floor. All six hen-painted mugs as well as the plates lay scattered in pieces over the floor.

"Oh, bloody hell!" she cried aloud, irritated not so much about the mess but because the mugs had been the ones that Iris had gifted her the previous Christmas.

Simon returned just as she had finished clearing away the mess. Molly flew into his arms and began to sob. Over her shoulder he saw the broken mugs that he knew she had grown fond of.

"It's ok Mol, I'm sure we can get some more" he spoke reassuringly to her, coaxing her out of the kitchen and supporting her up the stairs to bed. He knew that Molly had drunk more cider than she was used to and that it was the cause of her being so tearful. He had seen this all before.

Molly sat on the side of the bed crying while Simon helped her to undress.

"I'm sorry Si, I don't mean to be like this, I love you so much" she grizzled, throwing her arms around his neck.

"It's ok Mol. You will feel better in the morning, just had a little more cider than you should have had."

It was not long before she was in bed and under the duvet. Turning over just once before Molly fell into a deep sleep. Simon quickly undressed and laid down beside her. He gently manoeuvred her onto her side as she began a soft rhythmic snoring sound. He smiled as he recalled that Molly always denied ever snoring.

"One of these days I will have to record you and then you will know how you don't ever snore" he spoke softly. "And I guess sex is out of the question tonight" he whispered again teasingly into her ear, not expecting any reply.

"Not tonight, Si, I'm so tired and I have a headache or at least I will in the morning I suspect."

Chapter 4

Molly woke the next morning with the most terrible self-induced headache. Simon had left her a mug of coffee along with the customary two paracetamol tablets before taking Vanda for a walk. Blinking and wiping her eyes so she could focus more clearly, she looked at the mug which had her name painted on it and recalled what had happened the evening before. She sighed. Raising the mug to her lips she sipped the not so hot coffee and swallowed the pills that Simon had left for her. It would take Molly another half an hour before she could get out of bed to face the day ahead.

...***

It was no one's fault other than her own, thought Molly when she later went to gather the eggs and feed the chickens that morning.

The scene of destruction that surrounded her was tragic. She found the gate to the chicken pen was open. Molly remembered that she was the last one to see to the hens the day before. She had obviously forgotten to secure the gate.

Most of the chickens had gone. The rest had been cruelly mutilated and left scattered all over the ground. Molly began to cry. She dismissed the ugly thought of a coincidental accident of the previous evening when she had broken six hen-decorated mugs. Her tears flowed and she started to sob uncontrollably.

There had been only a handful of events in her life where she had allowed these sorts of emotions to take control. Molly had nearly always managed to maintain a stiff upper lip in times of crisis.

Molly knew she was stronger than the character she was displaying at this time and that her hormones were most probably to blame or at least contributed to the situation she found herself in. Using her hand and sleeves she began wiping away her tears. Slowing her breathing, taking in deeper breaths, and exhaling rhythmically until her sobbing ceased.

Somewhere from inside the hen house came a soft clucking sound. It was with a heavy heart and deep sadness combined with an overwhelming feeling of guilt that she approached the one remaining living hen in the coup. Unlike the other hens this one had not ventured out from the hatchery. Instead, it lay quietly huddled in the corner of its little house and could not be tempted to come out when it heard Molly approach.

"Come on Hennie Penny" she called to it in a quiet voice as she tried to encourage the hen to come out. She wanted to see if the hen displayed any injuries. Molly thought it was highly probable that the hen would not have survived unscathed as the pitiful thing looked to be in shock.

From a small bowl she had been carrying Molly took out a handful of food scraps. The hen suddenly began to be inquisitive. At first it stood up and ruffled its feathers. Molly immediately noticed the hen had indeed sustained a severe injury. Both wings were damaged, and Molly could see bloodstains still wet stuck to its feathers.

"Oh, you poor thing" she said as the hen eventually plucked up courage and came towards her. Such was her surprise when she noticed the solitary egg it had been sitting on.

"You're a clever girl" she said as she lifted the warm egg from the bed of straw. She wondered how the hen had managed to get away from its attacker. Examining it again Molly knew that her remaining hen would also have to be destroyed.

Molly Munday's business depended on vast amounts of eggs. The fox attack on bonfire night would be a lesson she would not easily be able to forget.

Chapter 5

There was no time to grieve and a few days later, with the chicken pens repaired and secure, Molly and Simon purchased new hens. Molly knew it would take time for a new brood to settle in, so she found a temporary supplier of fresh free-range eggs for the interim.

Molly's sadness, however, would not go away. Simon and her friends tried hard to help her come to terms with her feelings. After a spate of arguments with her husband over trivial things Molly realised, she was going to need professional help. She knew Simon was only trying to help her, but his jokes and innuendos that he thought were amusing had the opposite effect on her mood.

"Perhaps you should give Colonel Sanders a call" he had suggested after the event, trying to lighten her mood.

"This is a cracking cake Moll" says Simon on another occasion as he cut himself a large slice of cake.

"I cannot say anything to you without getting my head bitten off. I feel I am treading on eggshells all the time."

And that was the final straw!

Dr Foster listened and took notes whilst Molly, embarrassed, fumbled to find the words to describe her feelings and started to cry. He knew Molly well and not just through her baking and community events. He had even ordered cakes from her for special occasions. This was not the happy go lucky Molly he had come to know.

The upshot of her appointment would see Molly prescribed anti-depressants.

Holly And Mistletoe

Chapter 1

The Christmas cake orders were in and for the first time since she had started her own business Molly had to turn customers away. This was something she had hoped she would never have to do. Still her phone kept ringing.

Molly was beginning to feel more like herself and was looking forward to the lead-up to Christmas. She had stocked up on ingredients and spent time drawing up plans for the baking days ahead. Listing orders in priority of collections and deliveries.

The evening before the first baking day Molly was preparing bowls of dried fruits and fresh peels ready to soak them in brandy. There had been no need for Iris to help her with this as Simon volunteered to help her weigh the different fruits and measure out the brandy. His hand was still sore so when he tried to help with the grating of the peel Molly suggested she take over.

Simon had his Molly back. She seemed more relaxed and was able to laugh and joke again. Their relationship as good as it ever was "or nearly" he thought to himself, watching her as they worked together.

It was while they were working in the office and discussing their Christmas plans that the phone in their kitchen rang. Simon went to answer it.

"Hello, Simon Munday here. Yes, I can hear you clearly. Oh, that's wonderful news. Let me get your mum. She's only in the …." Molly listened to the one-sided conversation. The word mum making her realise that their daughter was on the other end. She immediately stopped what she was doing and hurried to the telephone, grabbing it from Simon's hand.

"Hello darling. How are you?" she asks. Then a pause as Molly listens. Simon puts his ear close to the phone so he too can hear the conversation.

"Oh, that's wonderful news darling. We shall look forward to it. Yes, we can discuss details later and make plans. I am so excited" she says.

"We love you too" she says signing off, blowing kissing sounds down the phone before she hangs up.

Molly throws her arms around Simon.

"I love you so much Si. I am so excited" she says, her face beaming.

"I would never have guessed" Simon teased, holding her close to him and feeling the excitement too.

"I think we should start earlier to prepare. There is so much to organise. I think a list would be a good idea. Don't you?" says Molly before Simon has time to respond.

"We can sit down later tonight with a bottle of wine and make plans" she suggests.

Simon feels excited too at the prospect of having Laura and Cam come home for Christmas, but he is even more overjoyed to see Molly so happy. The very tonic she needed, he thought.

"That's a date then" he said, taking Molly in a ballroom hold and then waltzing her around the kitchen. "And I think we should order in some pizza to celebrate."

"Better get this fruit sorted first ready for me and Iris to make a start tomorrow" says Molly, pulling herself away from his hold reluctantly.

Iris arrived early the next morning eager to show Molly the Christmas cake decorations she had made. Once again Molly thought Iris had excelled herself. As well as a selection of the usual moulded figures of the season Iris had made pairs of golden bells with red ribbons and sprigs of holly with berries. All beautifully crafted in sugar.

"I know I say it every time but is there no end to your talent?"

Iris is also relieved to see Molly back to her old self.

"I can't take all the credit Mol you did a lot too."

"Only the simple ones we made a couple of weeks ago for the cupcakes," said Molly. "And no way can you compare them with these."

"I got so many ideas from the sugar craft fair. It was well worth the trip!"

Iris takes the lid off a third box to reveal a selection of various size snowflakes and Molly draws a breath. One of their customers had a specific request for a large snow cake for a centre piece.

"These are fantastic Iris. How did you manage It?" asks Molly as she examines the assorted sizes of exquisite white glistening flakes of sugar that look so real.

"If I'm honest they were a little harder than I expected, and I had several attempts before I was satisfied, but I think Lady Jacqueline will like them" says Iris. "Don't you think?"

"Like them! I am sure she will be over the moon with the finished cake" says Molly, turning to the page in the sketch pad detailing what they hoped to achieve for the grand cake.

Lady Jacqueline from the manor house was one of Molly's best private customers and had placed orders with

Molly's cupcakes from the start of her new business. This cake was to be the centre piece for her annual fundraising auction, so it had to be striking to look at. Because it had been for charity Molly had offered to make it at cost price.

"I really don't expect you to do that" Lady Jacqueline had told her as she described the sort of decorated cake that she had envisaged. "You are much too generous, but I am extremely grateful to you."

Molly and Iris admired the sketched drawings of all the Christmas cakes that they had to make, checking they had everything for the individual designs. Together with those decorations for the cupcakes they decided they had more than enough and with spares.

"I think this snow cake will be the best of the lot. I might have to place a bid for it then I can keep it" says Molly.

"Not if I bid higher than you, you won't" Iris replied playfully.

They laid out the pillars and discussed how they could best fix the snowflakes to give the all-important three-dimensional design for the cake.

"Best we get baking otherwise there won't be any cakes to decorate" suggests Iris.

"Coffee first" says Molly. "I've got some exciting news to share" she says, steering Iris out of the office and into her kitchen.

Iris observed Molly as she filled the kettle. She was smiling and humming Jingle Bells. There was colour in her cheeks and Iris thought to herself how she was looking younger than her fifty years. She was pleased to know that her friend was in a much happier place now but concerned that she was relying on anti-depressants.

Iris had on one occasion considered taking HRT, but she thought her symptoms less severe than Molly's. She still maintained that the cocktail of natural supplements she was taking seemed to give relief to the worst of her symptoms, and that she was coping.

"That's great news Mol" said Iris when Molly told her about Laura and Cam.

"When are they coming?"

"They need to work out the details. Both need to organise time off work then they can book flights," said Molly.

"I wonder what their exciting news can be" said Iris, humming the tune to the familiar wedding march.

"I don't want get my hopes up, but if I may use a cliché, it would be the icing on the cake so to speak" says Molly.

Molly and Iris spent the remainder of the day creaming and mixing by hand and machines. They whisked and folded in all the measured ingredients before filling the cake tins to bake. The larger of the two ovens held more cakes at a time so they used this one for the sponge cakes. The second oven set with a lower temperature was allocated for the fruit cakes. These taking more hours to bake meant that only two batches could be made in any one day.

Hours ticked by as the two women worked. Both contented with forthcoming family visits and sharing their hopes and dreams for the future, interrupted only by one phone call from a would-be disappointed customer due to their workload, and another from a scratch at the door when Vanda needed to go out for a wee.

It was getting dark by the time the last cakes came out of the oven. Simon poked his head in to say that Rob had arrived.

"Perfect timing," said Iris. "Tell him five minutes."

Closing the door on the office Molly and Iris went into the kitchen. On the table Simon had placed four glasses.

"I think we should have a celebration drink" he said, taking a bottle of champagne from the fridge.

"And what are we celebrating my dear" asks Molly, gloating as if she did not know.

"Life!" says Simon "And our friends and families."

Chapter 2

The first two weeks of December flew by. Baking and decorating cakes was in full swing. Two batches of Cupcakes were delivered to the bakery with an order for one more in the third week before Christmas. Another three orders were due to be delivered in that same third week. The larger traditional fruit cakes were collected early by individual customers with the remaining requesting to have theirs delivered. One of these was to Lady Jacqueline at the manor house and two more to be delivered to the vicarage.

"Lovely as ever" commented a cheery reverend Tom Cutler when he opened the door and saw the ladies standing there each holding a box containing a Christmas cake.

Molly wished he had been referring to the cakes, but he had not even seen those yet, so she doubted that was the case. His comments somehow always had two meanings. Louise, having heard her husband at the door, went to see who he had been talking.

"How wonderful" she exclaimed when the lids of the boxes were opened to view the two cakes.

"You must come in for sherry" she suggested. "It's traditional you know."

"Bit too busy I'm afraid and I'm driving" replied Molly, eager to get away.

"I understand from Simon that your daughter and her friend may be coming home for Christmas," said the vicar.

"I hope we will get to see them both. We have not seen Laura since she moved to France. No doubt she is a very independent lady -just like her mother I suspect! And equally as pretty! You could all come to our little Christmas drinks party. And of course, you too Iris."

"Thank you, vicar. That would be lovely," said Iris, who had not noticed Molly blushing and was itching to get away.

"I will have to see," said Molly. "Busy time and all that!"

Iris thought Molly's reply was strange but thought it best not to comment.

Walking back to the car Molly turned to Iris.

"I've a right mind to go to his party" she said to Iris, who was bemused by Molly's negative tone of voice. "I wonder what he will make of Laura's partner Camille?"

"Of course we must go. You always go and it will fun, I'm sure!"

Iris was becoming increasingly concerned over Molly's indifference towards the vicar. Whenever she had mentioned him in conversation Molly always tried to change the subject. On more than one occasion Iris had witnessed what she thought was an unusual fondness towards Molly by him. When she had tried to make light of this Molly had been bad-tempered.

"We will see! Got a lot on you know!" she said, forcing a smile and ending the discussion.

Molly and Simon each had different thoughts when it came to discussing the couple's exciting news. Molly hoped wedding bells were on the horizon while Simon thought the couple may be considering relocating back to England.

"Best we do not speculate darling" said Simon for fear that Molly might be disappointed.

"Either would be wonderful news to me," said Molly.

"Well not long now till we find out. Meanwhile we have a house to decorate and gifts to buy," said Simon.

"And I still have another batch of cupcakes to make as well and don't forget we have the charity fundraiser at the weekend to go to."

"Best we get started then. Up into the attic again! It seems like it was just yesterday when I packed the Christmas decorations away" Simon teased as he left to find the stepladder.

Chapter 3

Lady Jacqueline's Christmas charity fundraiser was something Molly enjoyed going to. A chance to dress up and mingle with people that she was unlikely to meet otherwise.

Haywood Manor was renowned for its festive decorations. The height of its ceilings allowed for at least twelve-foot Christmas trees which Molly was quite envious of. Of course, her ladyship was not responsible for the decorations as she could afford to hire professional people to do this for her. Every year there would be a different theme, and this year was no exception.

Admittance to the auction was by invitation only and strictly a black-tie event. Guests included local businesspeople and their partners along with a few dignitaries. Her Ladyship also used the occasion to invite her closest friends. Naturally, the Reverend Thomas Cutler and his wife, always had an invitation.

There were not many opportunities in Molly's social calendar to dress up, so she especially looked forward to this one. The first time Molly had been invited to this event was as a plus one with Simon. He had connections with Lady Jacqueline through the college where she was their patron.

The previous year, like this one was due to her own merit and Molly felt proud. This year Molly had no qualms about contacting her ladyship asking if she would include her new partner Iris, and Rob as her plus one, and this she had done. Indeed, her ladyship had been very apologetic at her oversight of the exclusion in the first instance.

So, Molly and Iris went shopping together for evening dresses and accessories for the occasion. Each making their own arrangements for appointments to the hairdressers. Molly had never been able to sway Iris to try her hand with Katie.

"I prefer to stick with Raymond. He has done my hair for years" she had insisted. "And I really enjoy the head and shoulder massage I get before he starts to wash my hair."

"I'm sure he has the most amazing pair of hands" said Molly, causing them both to giggle as she realised what she had said. "I mean his technique when he massages your head and shoulders."

"It is so relaxing" says Iris seriously. "And he explains the benefits to the scalp."

"Even so I think I will stick to my Katie" says Molly. "And any massaging I want I can get from Si."

***

"Wow!" exclaimed Iris as the four of them enter Haywood Manor. "It's stunning."

This year's theme was based on a winter wonderland. White frosted decorations combined with silver and gold ornaments hung magically from the ceilings. Every corner of the room hosting an individual snow theme. The two identical trees looked magical. Both displayed large white and silver baubles. Long flowing strands of blue and silver hung glittering over the branches. Behind the trees was a backcloth of a blue starry night that twinkled with lights.

"No wonder she insisted on the snow cake" said Molly, her eyes scanning the room. "Everything has such a wow factor doesn't it." Close your mouth, Iris!" she whispered in Iris's ear, seeing her partner awestruck.

"Think I have gone to heaven Mol! Never imagined it would be like this. Thank you for getting us in."

"No more my right to an invitation than my partner's."

Waiters moved around the room mingling with the guests and carrying silver trays with glasses of champagne. Simon and Rob took two glasses each.

Lady Jacqueline employed her own staff to be waiters. On their trays they carried a selection of hors d'oeuvre. Iris and Molly with a glass in one hand took one each with a free hand straight to their mouths so they could pick a second. Mary, a waiter for today, was also one of Lady Jacqueline's cleaners. She lived in the village and knew both Molly and Iris well.

"Not like the pigs in blankets and sausage rolls we are used to eh! Mary" whispers Iris, enjoying a third succulent morsel from Mary's tray.

"Try one of these" said Mary pointing to a half of a quail's egg with a yellow creamy topping. "They are delicious. I ate two back in the kitchen."

"I must say the food looks wonderful, who did she get to do the catering this year?" asks Molly.

"Someone called Mrs Edwards I think" Mary replied.

"Do you mean Pru Edwards?" Iris asks.

"Yes" came the reply. "Do you know her?"

From across the room Molly and Iris simultaneously notice Pru and Mike. She caught their eye and proceeded to cross the room to join them.

"She scrubs up well" said Iris with a mouthful of food.

"Hello everyone, isn't this lovely" said Pru while the men chat to each other off to one side.

"It's lovely to see you, and Michael" said Molly acknowledging Michael's hand wave across the room. "The food is really good."

"Thank you. I met her ladyship at the golf club. I did a small catering event for the club, and she was there presenting an award. We got talking about her fundraiser. She told me she had been let down by her usual caterers due to an illness and asked if I would be interested."

A waiter came towards them, and each took another glass of champagne as the three women continued to chat.

From across the room the sound of someone chinking a spoon against a glass brought the room to quiet. The Reverend Thomas Cutler, dressed in a white tuxedo suit which Molly thought made him look like a film star and very handsome stood with Lady Jacqueline on his arm. She wore a long fitted white sequin dress which befitted her perfectly slim and shapely figure. Standing closely together, anyone who did not know them might have been forgiven for thinking them to be a showbiz couple. Molly had a moment of (the colour green) and she immediately chastised her stupid thoughts. The vicar cleared his throat and began to speak setting out the formalities for the evening.

This was one occasion when Molly did not have to worry about the vicar's advances as he only had eyes for her ladyship. Being a widower, she relied on him as she had on previous occasions to be her escort and host for the evening. So, with his wife on one arm and Lady Jacqueline on the other, they led everyone into the dining room to inspect the lots and write down their secret bids. Molly thought how attractive Louise looked. She wore a sparkling turquoise evening dress with silver accessories. The vicar looked as if he was in his element. Quite smug, Molly thought.

The decorations in the second and smaller of the two grand rooms replicated the larger room but without the trees. The auction lots were displayed on a long table which had been decorated by Lady Jacqueline herself. There were gold envelopes containing gifts, alternating with material gifts, as in one of two cases of champagne and a patchwork quilt which Molly knew the vicar's wife had made and donated. Each lot displayed with a surround of sparkling decorations. Silver baubles with lot numbers had been placed in front of them. In the centre of the table stood Molly and Iris's winter snow scene Christmas cake. Made by them and donated by Lady Jacqueline.

"It looks fabulous! Don't you think so Iris?" said Molly.

"It most certainly does. One of our best I think" said Iris, taking Molly's hand and giving it a gentle squeeze.

They separated, circulating around the room conversing with other people they knew. A small queue had gathered at the table, taking turns to place their bids. Having secured their bids, they then moved away making room for others to place theirs. Molly, seeing a gap, saw an opportunity to move forward to place her own bid.

"I hope you are not thinking of bidding for your own cake" came a familiar voice from behind her.

"No of course not!"

Molly did not see the vicar sidling up to her and she felt her pulse begin to race.

Why did he always manage to have that effect on me? Molly took a step back from his closeness.

"Why would I do that vicar when I can have cake anytime I choose" she said haughtily to him.

"That is all right then because I have my eye on that one. I do so wish you would call me Tom, Molly. We have been friends for an exceptionally long time, and sometimes even closer!" He whispered the last of those words so no one could hear him.

Iris, seeing them talking, saw that Molly had a look of concern. She thought she might need an excuse to get away so moved quickly towards them.

"Can I get there to place my bid?" she said, putting herself between them. The vicar smiled before reluctantly moving away and went to join his host in the adjoining room.

"I'm sure he fancy's you Mol!"

"Don't be silly Iris you know he flirts with everyone! Let's place our bids then we can find another drink."

Molly had donated an afternoon of a one-to-one baking session to be arranged in the new year. She saw her donation and was pleased the way it had been displayed next to the snow cake. Having examined the lots Molly knew which lot she was going to bid on and decided not to tell anyone. Iris followed suit.

Molly helped herself to a third glass of champagne and took a sip. She was feeling a little tiddly. Mary came to her side carrying a tray of sweet treats and Molly took two to sample and was impressed.

Eventually the four friends were back together again. The chatter and laughter in the room had got noticeably noisier as more alcohol was consumed.

A second chink of glass, this time a little louder.

"Ladies and gentlemen. The bidding is now closed. In a few minutes we will be able to see who has secured their bids. So, for now enjoy another glass of bubbles courtesy of her ladyship and I will let you know when we are ready," said the vicar.

"I've placed a bid for a coaching session with a pro golf player" said Simon looking pleased with himself. "Doesn't say who the coach is but I thought it might be fun."

"That is good to know Si! Because so have I mate" said Rob grinning. "I wonder whose pockets are deeper though."

"That's typical" says Molly smiling at them.

"May the best man win then" said Iris jokingly.

"Did you place a bid Mol?" asked Simon.

"I did but it's a secret" says Molly, smiling and tapping the side of her nose.

"And did you place a bid on anything Iris?"

"I did and I'm keeping mine a secret too" said Iris doing the same.

Chapter 4

The week before Christmas Laura and Camille flew into Gatwick airport. Simon was there to pick them up. He had left Molly at home making final preparations for their daughter's homecoming. Every year Molly seemed to put up more Christmas decorations and this year it seemed there were to be even more. Even poor Vanda had to suffer the indignity of wearing a festive collar to meet the rest of the family.

Molly was in the kitchen preparing a joint of beef for a roast dinner that evening. This was one of Laura's favourite meals. Every few minutes she glanced out of the window to see if they were coming up the drive.

Having drunk two mugs of coffee the machine was empty so she decided to refill it in hope they would be home soon. Timing could not have been more perfect. The fresh coffee was ready, and she too was ready for another cup.

With Vanda close on her heels and barking with all the excitement Molly went out to meet the car. She managed to grab Vanda by his collar just as the car came to a standstill. Simon got out first and held the door for the pair to get out. Molly hugged them in turn and then hugged them both again. Her eyes moist with happy tears.

"I'm so excited to have you both home for Christmas" says Molly. "I have missed you so much."

"I missed you too mum" says Laura hugging her mother and kissing both her cheeks just as the French do. And you too Dad." Laura flings her arms around his neck again just as she did at the airport.

"And you too Camille" says Molly as she is being kissed again on both cheeks.

"Merci de m'avoir invité a dans votre charmante maison" says Cam.

"Vous êtes toujours le bienvenue ici Camille." Molly responds in French. "Vous ferez tous partie de notre famille maintenant et nous vous aimons tous les deux."

"English please Mum! Cam and I have decided when in England we will speak English and when we are at home we will speak in French."

Molly loved to converse in French when she had travelled to France. It was a language that she had learnt as a child. Her own father had spoken French fluently and had taught the language in the local secondary school. He had encouraged Molly from an incredibly early age, and she was grateful he had. Many of their holidays as she grew up had been spent in France. Whilst there the family had only spoken the French language.

"And you must be Vanda" said Laura bending down to pet the dog who by now was making it quite clear he was feeling left out of all this affection. "I've been looking forward to meeting you having heard so much about your escapades."

Camille in turn stooped to make a fuss of the dog.

"Come on in, I have just made some fresh coffee" says Molly ushering them inside the house. "Your father will get your luggage." Simon had already opened the boot and was taking out the suitcases.

"I hope you have made one of your chocolate cakes as well" says Laura smiling at her mother, knowing full well that she would have.

They were soon seated at the kitchen table. Each with cups of coffee and large slices of chocolate cake. Vanda was jumping up and pestering the newcomers and being firmly told to stay down.

Molly had so many questions she wanted to ask. She was keen to know everything about their wellbeing, their jobs, and their plans while they were home.

She told them about the vicar's invitation to his party which was being held the following day. They were both eager to attend this as well as catching up with old friends.

"Now, we really want to know what you have both been up too" says Laura, squeezing her father's hands. "And we want to see your new office mum, and you can tell us all about Molly's Cupcakes business."

It seemed to Molly that her daughter was in no hurry to share the important news that she had spoken about on the phone. During the conversation Molly tried to broach the subject by updating Laura on her old friends from the village. The ones that had married and now had children. It had been one of Laura's closest friends from primary school that had been married and had subsequently got divorced. Molly had heard this from someone in the hairdressers.

Every time she mentioned the word marriage Simon would give Molly a look of annoyance and he tried to steer the conversation onto a different subject.

"When you have both unpacked and settled in Mum can give you the tour and she can show you her portfolio," suggested Simon, bringing Molly's probing questions to a much-needed interval.

"It's all right Mum, I know you are dying to know our news. Shall I put her out of her misery Cam?" Laura took

Cam's hand. Smiling she winked at her and then looked to her parents.

"We want to get married!"

"Oh, my darlings!" Molly was so excited. She jumped to her feet to hug them both. "Such wonderful news. We are so happy for you both, aren't we Dad."

"It is the best Christmas present you could have given your mother and me of course. Champagne time!"

Having hugged them both and Molly too, Simon went to the fridge and took out a bottle of champagne. From the glass cabinet he took out four crystal champagne flutes.

Molly had a sort of inkling about what the news might have been but had kept her thoughts to herself, trying desperately not to get her hopes up. She now felt as if all her hopes and dreams were coming true. With her health improving and the business doing well this was, she thought, most definitely the icing on the cake!

Ever since Laura had come out and told them she was moving to France with Cam, Molly and Simon had talked often about the likelihood that one day they might consider getting married and make their partnership formal.

It had not been easy for Laura to tell her parents that she was in a lesbian relationship. She had been nervous and fearful that the news might threaten the close bond she had with her parents. There had been several opportunities when she had visited her parents but for one reason or another, she had felt unable to tell them. It was just two years ago when another of these visits had taken place and Cam had accompanied her. On this occasion Laura had been determined to tell her parents. It was her father who heard raised voices coming from her room she had shared with

Camille. He heard her crying and knocked on the door. Laura loved her parents but had always found it easier to talk to her father ever since she was a child and especially during her teenage years. It was he who would eventually tell her mother.

Molly had been really upset. Not because Simon had told her that their daughter was a lesbian but because Laura had not felt able to tell her herself. This had really hurt.

"I just don't understand why she thought she could talk to you and not to me" she had said to him angrily. "I'm a good listener, aren't I?"

"Of course you are, well most of the time." He had tried to make a joke but looking at her face he wished he had not. Molly got terribly angry.

"And I am as liberal and unprejudiced as you, just look at some of our friends. Take Stu and Al for instance. When they came out, we were the first to embrace them and still call them good friends and Al's Laura's Godfather for goodness' sake."

"Not the same love when it's close family. Anyway, let me just remind you of the time when she had been caught smoking at school. Who did she come to then?"

"I know your right Si. I just wish that just this once that she had come to me first."

That was now all in the past and once it was out in the open her relationship with Laura was as strong and rich as ever.

Sipping champagne and looking at her daughter with Cam across the table, Molly could see two people very much in love. She wanted to bring up the subject of wedding plans but thought better of it. "Patience!" her thoughts echoed.

Having settled in and played with Vanda, Laura and Cam did the grand tour of Molly's office.

"Mum you are amazing. It is such a great workspace, and I am so jealous of all the fittings and equipment" says Laura, emphasizing the word equipment.

"You never know we might get some wedding gifts to add to our basic commodities in our kitchen back home" says Cam, smiling at her partner.

"You must come and look at Mum's portfolio" says Simon. "I'm in charge of the photography."

Laura and Cam sat on the high stools turning page after page studying the pictures. When it came to the photos of wedding cakes both let out sounds of" Wows!"

"Look at this one Cam" says Laura.

"I love this one" says Cam turning yet another page.

Molly thought, now I can broach the subject.

"Have you any ideas what you would like dears?

Laura looked at Cam, smiling, before turning to her parents.

"We know it is short notice mum and all that, but we want to get married as quick as we can. Please don't be cross with us but we have booked a registrar and office for the new year, and we have a wedding cake sorted" Laura tells her parents, knowing full well that her mother especially would be upset by the fact that they had already secured a wedding cake.

Both her parents are taken by surprise. Molly was even more taken aback and disappointed about the wedding cake news. On the other hand, she thought to herself, how would she have found time to make one unless they would settle for cupcakes?

"We really don't want a fuss, and we didn't want to burden you" says Cam. "We have booked an Airbnb for my parents and my brother and his wife to come here to share the day."

"We just need to find a suitable small venue for a reception," said Laura. "And I know how short notice it is but there is another reason for it."

Laura takes Cam's hand. "You see we are hoping to start a family and we have already put wheels in motion, so to speak."

Simon puts his arm around his wife. For once Molly is momentarily lost for words, her brain going into overdrive.

"I know!" says Molly suddenly. "I have a great idea. How about we have the reception here?" Turning to Simon: "We could do that couldn't we Dad?"

And so, it was gratefully accepted and agreed. Molly could not have been happier. Not just a wedding but a future with a grandchild as well. Everything for which she had hoped.

Chapter 4

The following evening Molly and Simon, with their daughter, prepared for the Christmas party at the vicarage.

"This will be fun" said Molly to Simon as she was putting on her makeup for the occasion. "Can't wait to see his face when we introduce Laura and her fiancée to him."

"Should be interesting" agreed Simon. "Not sure what his feelings are regarding same-sex marriages."

Molly was pleased that Iris and Rob had been included in the invitation. If ever she needed her best friend at her side, it would be on this occasion.

They had been delighted to hear of Laura and Cam's news. Molly had approached both Iris and Pru to see if they would be free in the new year to help her with the wedding reception. Both friends excitedly accepted.

The weather was turning colder, and a biting wind was blowing in from the east. The weather forecaster had warned of snow showers, to higher ground.

"I wonder if it will be a white Christmas," said Laura. "It would be even better if we had snow for our wedding wouldn't it Cam?"

"Better not get our hopes up. On the other hand, it would be a disaster if my family could not get across from France because of snow."

Wrapped in warm coats and with Simon driving they soon arrived at the vicarage.

"How pretty the garden looks" Laura commented. "All those fairy lights, it looks magical."

"Yes," agreed her mother, "magical! The vicar loves his fairy garden. Doesn't he dear" she said to Simon, squeezing his hand as they shared a private joke.

The vicarage porch was also decorated with fairy lights. A large holly wreath hung on the old-fashioned wooden door. Above this hung a large bunch of mistletoe tied with a red ribbon.

Louise answered the door, inviting them in, and Molly was grateful it had been her and not the vicar. If it had been him, he would have undoubtedly insisted on kissing everyone under the mistletoe, she thought to herself, and this she did not want him to do. At least not to her.

Several guests had already arrived. Molly looked across the room. She saw Iris and Rob were already there enjoying a glass of sherry. They were in conversation with the vicar. A small wave of acknowledgement from Iris, and the vicar turned round to see them. In his hand he held a sprig of mistletoe and Molly's heart started to race as he held it above his head and walked towards them.

"Customary you know" he said, stepping forward to plant a kiss on firstly Laura and then Cam before turning his attention towards her. Molly felt his warm lips on her cheek and momentarily froze. She took a step back. The vicar frowned and then smiled. "Welcome to you all and bless you for coming" he says, shaking Simon's hand.

"Of course, vicar, you know our Laura, and this is..." starts Molly proudly with the introduction.

"Actually, Molly, we have already met haven't we Cam?" he said, kissing both girls once again on their cheeks. "Albeit face to face online."

Molly is taken aback and more than a little disappointed that her plan to shock him had not worked.

"Forgot to say Mum. We contacted Reverend Cutler for advice about our wedding and asked him not to say anything until we had everything sorted. Did not want to spoil the surprise! Did we Cam?"

"Bless you both" said the vicar before he turns towards Molly and Simon. "They understand why I cannot officiate at their wedding, but I have offered to come along and say a prayer at their reception. That of course is if I am invited."

"Of course, you and your wife must come too" says Laura before Molly has time to think of an excuse not to invite him.

"Well, that's settled then," he said smiling at Molly. "Now you must help yourselves to drinks and some food" he says, "while I go and greet the rest of my guests."

Laura took Cam by the hand across the room where she had recognised the vicar's son who was with his girlfriend. There were other guests that she recognised and was keen to show off Cam.

"You've gone very quiet Mol, are you ok" asks Simon, concerned.

"Yes, I'm ok. Just a bit taken aback after that conversation" she replied. "Get me a large one will you."

It was turning into a merry Christmas party. The hosts having made everyone feel welcome. Lady Jacqueline arrived. The vicar swept across the room as she made her entrance and greeted her with a kiss. From then on, all his attention was taken up by this one important guest. For this Molly was grateful.

Across the room Molly watched her daughter. She and Cam looked so happy. They were talking to the vicar's son Daniel and his girlfriend having hugged them both. The vicar's younger son Alex they had been informed was away working in the states and could not get home for Christmas.

Molly thought how Laura and Daniel had displayed similarities in their appearance. Both tall and handsome. This however was where it stopped. Laura had her mother's dark hair where Daniel was as fair as both his parents.

Being of the same age Molly had watched them as they both grew up. Every time Molly had observed a mannerism, Laura and Daniel equally possessed she had dismissed this as coincidence. They had not been close friends since their primary years, which Molly had been pleased about. When they had chosen different educational paths and had gone to their respective universities, she had been relieved. She believed that as young adults it was best that they did not share too much time together.

Molly swallowed the last of her sherry as Iris approached.

"Penny for them!" says Iris, seeing what she thought was a look of melancholy on her friend's face. "Are you ok?"

"I'm fine thanks" says Molly. "In fact, I couldn't be happier" she says, smiling and pointing to her daughter.

"Want another one?" Iris asks, showing her own empty glass.

"Yes, please, why not. It is Christmas!"

"And when it's all over we will get together and organise their wedding," says Iris. "We will have at least a week, won't we? And we have proven repeatedly how well we can manage."

"We certainly can Iris. Not just best friends but best co-workers too" she said.

Iris takes Molly's glass to refill it. Molly once again looks across at her daughter who looks as happy as any bride should be. To Molly's left she saw Simon with Rob and Mike. Simon caught her eye. He smiled and winked at her, raising his glass. Molly could not hear their conversation but imagined the banter between them as Mike would be boasting about his winning bid for the golf coaching, he had won. Both she and Iris had put bids on the snow cake, but they had both been outbid.

This was going to be the best Christmas ever thought Molly. As for the new year she had a wedding to look forward to, and as for grandchildren she was prepared to wait a while but hopefully she thought not for too long.

The future of Molly's Cupcakes looked promising. The small business had far exceeded all her expectations.

It had been rumoured that the little tea shop in the village was closing shortly. Molly had not dismissed this as a possible new year project.

***

This Christmas especially, and this evening, was not the time to dwell on that incident all those years ago when Molly had made the biggest mistake of her life. The mistake that kept coming back to haunt her.

It was just that one time when she had let down her guard, had got drunk and had sex with a vicar. Simon had been away, and Tom wearing his collar had paid a call on his old school friend, welcoming her back to the village. He bought with him a bottle of wine. As old acquaintances she saw no reason not to invite him in. One bottle of wine led to a second and then to a third. They reminisced about their past and how they had both fancied one another.

There could be no blame on either party as both took an equal willingness to enjoy each other's body. Thomas left in the early hours before she woke. How he got home and the explanation he had given his new wife she could only imagine.

Neither of them had ever spoken of that evening again. Molly liked to think that Tom had never really remembered the occasion. If he had he had never in all the years past mentioned it to her. Molly thought that she would never know, and really had no wish to. She inwardly smiled to herself before turning her head to see Iris returning carrying two large glasses of sherry, one in each hand.

***

Laura and Cam's wedding cake turned out to be none other than the snow cake that she and Iris had made and donated to Lady Jacqueline's silent auction. The reverend Thomas

Cutler had told Laura and Cam about it, explaining that as they were getting married in the new year, that they might like to consider putting in a bid. Laura thought this was such a lovely idea and would delight her mother so had agreed. The vicar secured the bid on their behalf.

As for the donation gifted from Molly for a one-to-one baking session with Molly in her kitchen, the Reverend Thomas Cutler had secured the bid for himself and was greatly looking forward to the new year for this. Molly was not!

The End